THE RATTLESNAKE CODE

Tim Hogan and Gerard DuBois were childhood friends in antebellum Georgia, but their lives took very different paths after the Civil War, with DuBois becoming an outlaw and Hogan a deputy marshal. Now, in 1890, both men are middle-aged — and Hogan is charged with hunting down the companion of his youth. But neither man is prepared to abandon his honour just to win the battle — come what may, they will still adhere to the rattlesnake code.

ED ROBERTS

THE RATTLESNAKE CODE

Complete and Unabridged

LINFORD
Leicester

First published in Great Britain in 2015 by
Robert Hale Limited
London

First Linford Edition
published 2018
by arrangement with
Robert Hale
an imprint of
The Crowood Press
Wiltshire

A catalogue record for this book is available
from the British Library.

ISBN 978–1–4448–3560–1

Published by
F. A. Thorpe (Publishing)
Anstey, Leicestershire

Set by Words & Graphics Ltd.
Anstey, Leicestershire
Printed and bound in Great Britain by
T. J. International Ltd., Padstow, Cornwall

This book is printed on acid-free paper

Prologue

For much of the nineteenth century, no official legal apparatus of any kind operated across wide swathes of the United States. There were no court-houses and the nearest peace officer could be a couple of days' ride away. You might have thought that this was a perfect recipe for unbridled licence, where mayhem and murder would run unchecked.

Men cannot live so; at least not for long. A set of rules was developed to discourage, if not wholly prevent, wanton bloodshed and random murder. When folk found themselves living beyond the reach of ordinary courts, they devised their own system; one suited to that time and place. The men in those days put together and adopted a code of honour which was as rigid in its own way as the rules of medieval chivalry.

1

The aim of this system was to limit bloodshed and to ensure that when violence did take place, it was to some extent regulated. The consequence was a few basic and unbreakable rules. You could not shoot a man unawares, without giving warning of your intentions; you must not kill a man after eating his bread and accepting his hospitality; you could not smile at a man and then the next second attack him with lethal force; women and children were sacrosanct; priests and places of worship were to be respected.

This set of rules was accepted by good men and bad, alike. The essential feature was that you always signalled an intention to strike and eschewed such cowardly practices as shooting a man in the back or ambushing him unexpectedly from cover. They named this set of rules after a creature familiar in the lonely and uninhabited parts of the West — one which always gave fair warning before an attack. These conventions became known as the Rattlesnake Code.

1

4 August 1856

Two boys of about eleven or twelve years of age were playing together down at the creek near the little town of Fisher's Landing. You could tell at a glance that one of the lads was pure Georgia Cracker. Even at that tender age, he had that pale and washed-out look about him that is typical of the breed. The other boy was a harder study. He was swarthy and dark; his head topped with a mass of lustrous black curls. You might have taken him for Spanish or Mexican, but in fact his parents were French. His name was Gerard DuBois and his father owned the biggest plantation in the county. His companion was called Tim Hogan and the two of them were currently engaged in trying to dam up a little stream which ran into the creek. They had taken a break from this exhausting enterprise and were now sitting on the bank, pitching stones into the water.

'When I'm growed up,' said Gerard, 'I'm going to be the richest man in the whole of Georgia.'

'M'pa, he say that there's more important things in life than just money,' said the other boy. 'He say as bein' decent and keepin' faith is worth more'n all the gold in the whole, entire world.'

'He only says that,' observed his friend shrewdly, 'because he's not likely to have a heap of gold. Being faithful and decent don't cost anything.'

Tim Hogan laughed. 'I'll allow there may be somewhat in that,' he conceded. 'C'mon, let's finish a dammin' o' this here stream.'

29 October 1890
'Beau' DuBois was in constant pain from the rheumatics and it was proving a regular trial to him. Too many nights

spent in the cold and damp over the years, evading those who would do him harm, had taken their toll on his health. Now there are ailments from which the leader of a gang of outlaws might legitimately suffer, without risking any loss of dignity. Shiver with the ague for a spell or turn yellow for a day or two with fever and your men will sympathize and wish you a speedy recovery. Only once admit though, that you are feeling unwell all the time and that moreover your behind is aching damnably from the chill weather, and you might as well give up banditry at once, for good and all. That's how it is when you ride on the wrong side of the law; strength, daring and physical health are everything. Nobody is likely to follow a sickly weakling.

The consequence was that DuBois kept quiet about the misery in his back and the only sign he gave that things weren't right with him was that his temper was a little shorter and his language a mite fouler than usual.

Really though, he had good cause for being a little irritable that afternoon, even without the added aggravation of aches and pains. For the better part of a week, Beau and his boys had been remorselessly pursued by a posse which seemed to have almost superhuman determination, combined with an uncanny knack for keeping on their trail. They were like coon-dogs, sticking to DuBois and his men over a distance in excess of two hundred miles. This meant that he and his gang had hardly dared sleep for over a week, lest they woke to find themselves captives. Now, high up in a pine forest on the side of a mountain in Arkansas, just when Beau DuBois had hoped that they had shaken off their pursuers, one of his men reported that a horseman was heading up the track in their direction.

Speaking in general, men find it a good deal easier to slide down than they do to rise up. Slipping into degradation and low ways often happens almost as a matter of course with many people; whereas climbing to greater things and improving yourself requires a definite effort of the will. After the end of the war, Gerard DuBois returned to Georgia to find that his old way of life no longer existed. The plantation was overgrown, the house burned to the ground by the Yankees and the slaves all gone; freed by Mr Lincoln. Some men in similar positions started farms or businesses; they worked hard and prospered. Young DuBois who was barely twenty years of age on his discharge from the army lacked the willpower and moral fibre for such an arduous course of action. Instead, he took up as a road agent; an enterprise that in another era would have made him a highwayman.

There was a time when Beau DuBois and his gang were the terror of three states. They robbed trains, held up stages, knocked over banks and were seldom out of the headlines. Years passed though, and after a lengthy stretch in the penitentiary, DuBois was no longer the lively young rascal that he had once been. The glossy, blue-black curls were now a steely grey and he was coming up fast towards the age of forty-six.

The rider entered a clearing which lay some hundred and fifty feet below the spot DuBois and his men were camped. The man in the saddle looked round and gave the impression that he was sniffing the air like a dog in search of a trail. DuBois watched the fellow intently, and then experienced an almost physical jolt as he realized who it was. The man next to him cocked his rifle and sighted carefully down the barrel. Without even turning round to face him, DuBois swept his right hand upwards, knocking the barrel aside. He muttered fiercely, 'Don't you even think on it!'

The rider down in the clearing appeared to have lost the scent that he was seeking. He turned his horse and then trotted back the way he had come.

Beau DuBois turned to the man at his side and said, 'What ails you? You think to gun down a man while he is unawares? I'll have no scurvy tricks of that sort by any man as rides with me.'

'But Beau,' protested the other, 'he was almost on us.'

'Yes, you damned fool, and what effect would your rifle shot have had? It would have brought the rest of the boiling about our ears in no time. You'd have acted like a cowardly assassin and then brought us all under the shadow of the noose at the same time.'

It was this mixture of idealism and the eminently practical which made Beau DuBois such a well-respected leader of outlaws. He was, according to his lights, as straight as a die and a man of honour. He was also the most ruthless of individuals when it came to acquiring other folk's money and property, having a happy facility for divining where cash money, gold, jewellery and other portable goods were to be found and the means by which they could most easily be parted from their legitimate owners.

There were currently five members of

the DuBois gang hiding out with him up in the Ozarks. Long ago, in his youth, DuBois had picked up the sobriquet 'Beau', because he was so smooth, well-dressed and good-looking. These days, he was known to one and all as Beau DuBois. Almost invariably, those who talked of him pronounced 'DuBois' in the English manner as 'Do boys'.

★ ★ ★

After the War between the States, Tim Hogan had tried his hand at various lines of work, ranging from bartending to buffalo hunting. After a while, he had drifted quite naturally into law keeping. He had never had the desire to seek office, being quite content to remain a deputy marshal until the time came for him to hang up his gun. After working in different states, he had settled in a small Missouri town called Jacob's Lot, which was about thirty miles west of St Louis.

By 1890 almost everywhere east of

Kansas City was as quiet and respectable as the most peaceful country in Europe. There might still be bushwhackers and bandits up towards Wyoming and Nebraska and maybe a few in the Indian Territories, but in and around St Louis, things were as civilized as you could wish. Until that is, the DuBois Gang came riding in, having found that the former Indian Territories of Oklahoma had become a little warm for them. A nice, well-ordered city like St Louis must have looked to those boys like a sheep just waiting to be sheared and relieved of its coat. They lit in, robbed a bank and then almost immediately went after a high-class jeweller's store. The storekeeper kept a sawn-off scattergun under the counter and that little venture turned into a running gun-battle along the street in which stood the biggest and finest hotel in the city.

This was at a time when the mayor of St Louis was promoting his town as being the ideal stopping-off place for

11

folk from Europe travelling with Thomas Cook's. Other cities were becoming wealthy through tourism, so why not St Louis? It was a grand scheme, but the arrival of the DuBois Gang cast rather a blight upon the whole thing. All those visitors from France and England might be pleased enough to see a bunch of shooting at Buffalo Bill's Wild West Show, but they didn't take to getting caught up in such goings on in the street outside their hotel!

The mayor was not without influence and so a few days later, Tim Hogan was summoned to the marshal's office, who asked him, 'You got anything much on at the minute, Hogan?'

'No, chief. One or two lots of papers to be served, but nothing as can't wait.'

'You hear about 'Beau' DuBois' latest little exploit?'

'I did,' said Hogan grimly. 'But that was away over in St Louis. How's it come to be our affair?'

'Word is, DuBois and his men are heading this way and are likely to pass a

12

few miles to the south of Jacob's Lot. Could you get some men together and try and take him?'

Tim Hogan thought this proposal over for a spell, before saying, 'You mind that I know DuBois? He and I were boys together before the war.'

'I heard,' said the Marshal. 'Would that make it a problem for you to go after the man?'

Tim Hogan shook his head and said mildly, 'No, I reckon not.'

Which accounts for how the posse was chasing Beau DuBois and his gang across Missouri and up into the Arkansas Ozarks. The only problem was that all the men Hogan had been leading had lives and businesses of their own to pursue. It was one thing taking up like this and being paid a daily retainer to help catch somebody, but after a week, those fellows had had enough. Hogan found it enormously frustrating: he knew in his waters that DuBois was just a couple of miles away, like as not hiding in some forest. He couldn't persuade the men to come any further though, and every one of them dug up and headed back across the state line into Missouri. That was how Tim Hogan came to ride up into that pine wood alone and damned near get himself shot for his troubles.

★   ★   ★

After DuBois had watched Tim Hogan ride off, back the way he had come, he got to his feet and returned to where his men were sitting around disconsolately. It was a damp, grey day and nobody had been best pleased when he had forbidden them to light a fire to warm themselves a little. What a mercy though, he thought now, that he had insisted upon that precaution. A wisp of smoke above the treetops or the faintest hint in the air of the smell of burning pinecones would have had them surrounded in a flash.

The pain in his buttocks was now spreading down into his thigh. DuBois knew without a shadow of doubt that he had to get back indoors, at least for a month or two. He'd be a cripple for life if he let this go on much longer.

'Well boys,' announced DuBois, 'I've an idea as those wretches who have been chasing us for so long, have lost the trail now. And speaking for myself, I want to rest up for a spell before getting up to any more high jinks.'

There were wry smiles and nods of reluctant agreement to these sentiments. These men didn't live up in the mountains like wolves and bears; all of them had homes to go to when they had had enough of being on the scout. This happened periodically; often, as in the present case, when they came within a whisker of being caught.

'You think a month might be enough?' asked one of the men.

'I reckon so,' replied DuBois. 'They must be mighty ticked off in St Louis to set the bloodhounds on us to chase us all the way up a tree here. We need to let things die down a little.'

'You going home?' said somebody else. 'Or are you heading to that farm of yours?'

'Farm first,' said DuBois. 'I mind that somebody might set a watch on my home. I don't want to track mud to her door.'

Beau DuBois' wife and son lived in the east of Arkansas, but he had a little farm that he used when he needed to hole up and stay away from home. This was no more than a smallholding where he grew a few vegetables and lived peaceably. Not one person in the district knew that Frank Butler, the quiet, middle-aged man who was so often off travelling on vague and unspecified business was really none other than Beau DuBois, the famous outlaw.

'You men best not throw your money around and attract attention to yourselves, you hear what I say?' said DuBois. 'Just let things settle down a mite before you start buying your girlfriends geegaws and baubles and suchlike.'

There were chuckles when DuBois

said that. The previous year, a new member of the gang had no sooner got home than he had been chucking his money around like a drunken cowboy. He was now serving fifteen years in the federal penitentiary.

★ ★ ★

Tim Hogan was the mildest and most agreeable of men, but he didn't like being made a fool of any more than the next fellow. He knew very well that Gerard DuBois had been up in those pine woods with his friends and that they were most likely laughing now at seeing him baffled and his efforts to catch them set at naught. This, together with the fact that his posse had all deserted him and cut and run for home, had instilled in Deputy Hogan a fervent desire to track down his childhood friend and show him that he would not, after all, have the last laugh. Maybe it wasn't merely an impartial wish for justice to be served which prompted these thoughts in Hogan. It

17

was entirely possible that incidents from their early life together still rankled in him.

The Hogans had been dirt poor; next door, in the eyes of some in that part of Georgia, to white trash. DuBois, on the other hand, was from a family who were as rich as Croesus and as proud as Lucifer. Gerard DuBois had, not unnaturally, inherited some of that pride and contempt for others who were less fortunate than he himself. He had been fond enough of his playmate, who lived in a mean little cabin on the edge of Fisher's Landing, but from time to time, he made sure that Tim Hogan was aware of the gulf that separated them socially. Thirty five years later, the sting of this had not wholly faded and perhaps the deputy federal marshal was all the keener to run down DuBois for that very reason. Be that as it may, no sooner had he got back to Jacob's Lot than he went to see his boss and asked permission to spend some time tracking down Beau DuBois by himself.

'What's that?' asked Marshal Granger. 'Why should I let you go haring off on a snipe hunt like that? Is this some personal grudge?'

Hogan shrugged, which provoked an angry response from his superior, who said, 'Don't you shrug at me like that. It ain't respectful and I won't have it.'

'It'd be a right feather in your cap if we were the ones to catch Beau DuBois and break up his gang,' said Hogan. 'Set you in good favour with the folk in St Louis too, I dare say.'

'Yeah, I already thought on that. How long d'you reckon it'd take you?'

'Happen I'd be back here in a fortnight. Maybe a bit longer. I'd keep in touch though.'

Marshal Granger tapped his teeth with his pen; a trick of his when he was thinking hard. At length he said, 'Yeah. Go ahead and do it. You bring in DuBois and it'll do us both some good.'

'Thanks, chief,' said Hogan, 'I right appreciate this. I don't think you'll regret it.'

2

DuBois didn't have a long ride to his smallholding. It lay near the foothills of the Ozarks, not far from Little Rock. As he trotted along, he thought about Tim Hogan. It's curious how different two men's memories can be of the same sequence of events, even when both are trying to be as honest as they can and not dissemble. From all that Gerard DuBois was able to collect, he had always been pretty good to the Cracker with whom he had shared many childhood adventures. He had never lorded it over Tim Hogan, the way that some in his position might have been tempted to do. As far as DuBois was concerned, they had practically been equals. Why, he had shared what he had with the other boy, even down to giving him money from time to time. No, he didn't need to reproach himself with having treated the poorer lad badly at all.

That was one of the reasons that he had knocked Mike Sweeney's rifle up when he saw that the man was about to fire at his old, childhood friend. Of course, he would most likely have done so in any case. He hated to see any violation of the Rattlesnake Code. It was the one set of values that he still held dear. He had long since abandoned his Bible-learning and most of the rules of civilized society, such as those touching theft and murder, for example. But he had never yet breached the old code and what's more, he never would, not while he had breath in his body.

It had taken him right back to his early years to see Hogan there. He had come across the man during the war, of course, and had heard of him from time to time since then. Funny, to think of good old Tim being a lawman now! Somebody had pointed him out last year when he was passing through

Missouri. The man who had drawn attention to the deputy had mentioned that Hogan was known to be as straight as could be and impossible to bribe. As Tim Hogan walked past, DuBois had studied him carefully; noting the changes that the years had wrought in his face. And now the famous deputy had turned up looking for him.

While he was musing in this way, DuBois gradually became aware of something happening ahead of him. He was moving along a track through a little wood and because the path in front of him twisted and turned he could only see as far as the next bend. There were muffled oaths from a man and then, to DuBois' surprise, a woman's voice cried, 'Oh help, please don't hurt me!' At once, he spurred on his horse and cantered forward to see what was what.

The scene that met DuBois' eyes was one calculated to arouse his fiercest passions. Two men were struggling with a pretty young girl of about eighteen or nineteen. She had evidently been riding in her buggy, for this was standing nearby, on the track. Two villainous looking men, one black and the other white, were manhandling her now in a way which left DuBois in no doubt as to their intentions. There were no horses nearby, other than the one hitched up to the buggy and so it looked as though these boys had simply jumped out from the bushes, hoping to rob some passing traveller. DuBois had no problem at all with such a course of action; he had done the same thing himself and that more than once. This was something else again though. You did not, if you were a real man, lay hands on a woman in this way.

Gerard DuBois reined in his horse, it took him less than a second to interpret the tableau which he saw in front of him. The black man saw him first and turned to face him, while his partner kept ahold of the young woman. 'You know what's good for you, you gonna keep on ridin' past,' said this man. He didn't appear to be armed and so DuBois ignored him and called instead to the man with his hands on the girl:

'You had best let go of that young lady. Just release her and step back.'

The man did not let go of the girl, but twisted his head round to face DuBois, saying, 'It's no affair of yours. Are you the law?'

'Nothing of the kind,' said DuBois, smilingly. 'Just happened to be passing by. Are you going to let her go?'

Thinking back on the business later, DuBois couldn't see that any of what next chanced had been his fault. He had spoken plainly to those two men and all that they needed to do was follow his instructions. Had they done so, nobody needed to get hurt. What actually happened was that the black fellow pulled a knife from a sheath at the back of his belt and came charging towards DuBois. The mounted man didn't hesitate for a moment; simply pulled the pistol at his hip and shot the man down like the dog he was. The gunfire startled the other man and this gave the girl the opportunity to bite him hard on the hand that he had gripping the front of her dress. Then she pulled away from him and ran to DuBois for protection.

There was something almost comical about the expression on the fellow's face, as it slowly dawned on him that his partner was dead and he had no hostage to bargain with. DuBois pointed his gun at the man and said, 'I ought to kill you too, you know that?'

'I ain't done anything!' whined the man fearfully.

'It wasn't for want of trying though, was it?'

'You a-goin' to shoot me?'

DuBois looked at this pathetic excuse for a man and then said, 'Ah, be off with you now. I see you again, you better say a prayer.'

After the second assailant had scuttled off, DuBois dismounted and said to the girl, 'You all right, miss?'

'I am. Thank you. Lord knows what

would have become of me had you not fetched up. I am right grateful.'

'It's nothing. I'm glad I could be of service. You live near here?'

'Of course I do. You don't recognize me, Mr Butler?'

He looked more closely at the girl and then said, 'To be sure. You're Ned Archer's daughter, are you not? Jane? I'm sorry, I don't have all that many dealings with my neighbours. Of course I see who you are now.'

'You've been away for a while.'

'Yes, I've been on a business trip. I'm back for a few weeks now though. Come, let's get you back into the buggy and I'll escort you home. It's madness for an unprotected woman to be out riding in a lonely spot like this. I can't think what your father is about letting you do it.'

'Oh, please don't scold me, Mr Butler.'

DuBois could see that despite her bold words and air of affected indifference to what had befallen her, the girl was quite shaken up and so he said no more. He handed her into the buggy and then went back towards his horse. She called out, 'What about yon fellow? We can't just leave him there, surely?'

'Should I put him in the buggy with you?'

Jane Archer shivered and said, 'Don't say so. Really, do you mean to leave him there?'

'Maybe when I get to your father's house, I'll tell him about it all and he can take any steps he feels are needful and fitting. I surely am not aiming to dig a grave for this rascal, nor get the parson to deliver a eulogy, either.'

★ ★ ★

What Tim Hogan hadn't seen fit to let his boss know was that in order to track down Beau DuBois, Hogan was quite willing and able to commit a federal offence himself. He didn't think for a second that DuBois was going to trot straight back to his wife and son having narrowly escaped capture at the hands of that posse. No, he would hole up somewhere for a spell and then try to make contact by arranging to meet her somewhere. Well, that was fine. Assuming that they weren't communicating by telegraph, then Pauline DuBois and her husband would most likely be writing to each other by regular mail. All Hogan needed was to catch a glimpse of the address of any letters that DuBois' wife was sending and he would be sure to get a line on his man.

November was just round the corner and it was turning sharp. Hogan buttoned up his jacket against the wind which had begun to blow from the east. It was a fair ride from one end of Arkansas to the other, but it would be worth it. Tampering with the federal mail service was not the kind of thing that you can ask a man to do on your behalf. He thought that once he showed his badge in the post office, the clerks there would see how it was and let him peek at the mail without too many questions.

The wind whistled through Jacob's Lot and Tim Hogan tucked his head down and made off towards the livery stable. If it was cold here, Lord knows what it would be like up in the mountains! Hogan was riding the first few miles of his journey with Tyler Maddocks, the other deputy marshal in the town. Maddocks was the closest thing that Hogan had to a friend, these days. Tim Hogan had always been a solitary kind of man and had never married. The older he got, the more folks used to joke that he was married to his job and that this left no room for a woman in his life. There was some truth in this. He had never been overly successful with women and found the companionship of men every bit as satisfying as he imagined being cooped up in a house with a woman all day would be. Hogan had certainly never felt the lack of a wife.

Maddocks greeted him cheerfully, saying, 'Granger went for it then? You're off to roam round Arkansas on a fool's errand, while I do all the donkey work here? Well, I guess that's life.'

'You think chasing Beau DuBois up hill and down dale at this time o' year'll be like a Sunday School outing? I don't think so.'

'No,' said Maddocks. 'But still and all, you must admit as it'll make a pleasant change from serving subpoenas and such.'

'Maybe.'

The two men knew each other so well, that there was no need for a heap of pointless chatter as they rode south. Ten, fifteen minutes would pass without either of them speaking as they travelled along. At length, after neither man had spoken for almost twenty minutes, Maddocks said, 'So what is it with you and DuBois? They say he broke your heart, cut you out of some girl as you were sweet on.'

'You're a good friend, Maddocks, but sometimes you say too much,' observed Hogan. 'No, it's nothing like that. Fella's been dancing between the raindrops for too long, is all. Time he was brought down.'

'But you knew him when you was a kid,' persisted Maddocks. 'That's true, ain't it?'

'Yeah, that's true. Used to play together a whole lot when I was eleven or twelve.'

'He upset you in them days? That why you got such a down on him now?'

'No,' said Hogan, trying to be fair, 'I wouldn't say as he upset me none when I was a child. Let's leave it now, hey?'

'Just as you say.'

The two men rode on for another mile or so, before Tim Hogan said, 'I guess it just gets my goat that a man can carry on so all his life and act like he has the right to do so. When he was a boy, DuBois always acted in the self-same fashion, like he had the right to do as he pleased. Now he's lost everything, the plantation, the fortune and all the rest of it, but he still carries on the same way. I don't like it.'

31

Ned Archer expressed his gratitude to DuBois in no uncertain manner, for rescuing his foolish young daughter. To Jane, he said, 'Have you lost your mind, child? Riding up into those hills alone, without telling first where you was going? I'm more than half minded to take the buggy whip to you.'

'Ah, come on,' said DuBois. 'Weren't you young yourself once? Never do anything foolish? I surely did.'

Jane Archer shot him a grateful look. Her father said, 'Just get yourself in that house, miss, and make yourself useful to your ma.' He turned to DuBois and said, 'You'll stay for our evening meal, Butler?'

'Thanks, but I best be moving on.'

'No, I insist. I owe you. It's the least we can do. Come on.' He turned and began walking towards the farmhouse. It struck DuBois that if he were to snub this offer of hospitality, then it would set fair to raising bad feeling between him and a neighbour; which was the last thing he wished to do. With a sigh of irritation, he dismounted and led his horse towards the nearby field.

The Archers were amiable enough company, but DuBois was itching to get back to his own place. Mrs Archer said, 'Lordy, but we don't see much of you, Mr Butler. You live just over the hill there, but times are that we don't set eyes on you for a month or more at a stretch. Beats me how you manage to farm that land of yours.'

'I don't make a living by farming, ma'am,' said DuBois. 'Truth is, I only grow what I need for my own self. My real business lies in finance.'

'Do you work for a bank, Mr Butler?' asked Jane Archer artlessly, and DuBois almost laughed out loud at the thought. He restrained himself though and said gravely:

'It's a little more complicated than that, Miss Archer — stocks and securities and suchlike. It's mighty dull and I can't think any of you folks want to hear about interest rates and percentages. Have I missed anything while I been away?'

It appeared that life in the nearby farming community had progressed in the same, dull way since he had been gone as it usually did. The greatest excitement was that there were rumoured to be irregularities in the local church and a young curate was suspected of using the collection money for his own purposes. This was why Butler loved this area; it made such a pleasant contrast to his other life. At last, he said, 'Well, it's been nice visiting with you folks, but I'm afraid that duty calls. I have a mort of paperwork to catch up on and so I must bid you all goodnight.'

'Oh, don't go yet,' said Jane. 'Tell us what you are planning to do now, Mr Butler.'

'That's no secret,' he said. 'Although it's a little shameful and shocking.'

'Oh, do tell us. We don't hear nearly enough shocking news here.'

DuBois smiled. He was glad now that he had accepted Archer's invitation to eat with his family. Playful and light-hearted conversation of this sort was sadly lacking when one is hiding out in the mountains with a bunch of bandits. He said, 'Well, it's like this. I have developed an ailment in an unmentionable part of the body.' Mrs Archer looked scandalized and so DuBois hastened to make it clear what he meant. 'I am referring, of course, to that part of my anatomy which is used for sitting upon furniture and so on. In short, I have the rheumatics.'

Archer's wife clucked sympathetically. 'My, don't I just know what that feels like! I have a pot of goose fat that I can let you have, Mr Butler. You'll find that eases the pain somewhat.'

'It's a kind offer indeed ma'am and I am vastly obliged to you, but I have another plan. In three days' time, I'm setting off for Eureka Springs, to take the waters there. I hear where many have found their rheumatism all but cured at the place.'

'Why,' said Ned Archer, 'I mind

you're right about that. They call that town America's answer to Switzerland. There's a sanatorium or two up there, as well as the baths. I hope it does the trick for you.'

Archer went outside with DuBois as he fetched in his horse. When they parted, he said to DuBois, 'I owe you a big favour, Butler. You just call on me when you've a need.'

Someone from the village collected his mail for DuBois and brought it up to the house. Not that there was much of it. He hadn't seen Pauline and his boy for two months now, although he had made sure to send them more than enough money to live on. In her letters, his wife did not complain, but he detected a wistful longing in them; a longing partly for him and also for a normal life. Pauline had known what brand of man he was ten years ago, when they had married. She had known what he was but, like many women under such circumstances, thought that she could change him. The years since had shown her what a forlorn hope this was and DuBois thought that she had come now to accept who he was and what her life would in consequence be like.

Matthew, his son was nine now. DuBois knew fine well that he should be at home more with the boy, teach him how to be a man. The devil of it was though that after living this kind of life for over twenty years now, he knew no other. If he did give it all up and settle there with his wife and child, how would he keep them? Being raised as the pampered son of a rich plantation owner had not really fitted him out for any occupation that he could think of and he was getting a little old now to change his ways. What the future held, he tried not to think.

★ ★ ★

Hogan and Maddocks parted company at the point where one road went east and the other went south across the state line into Arkansas. Maddocks said, 'You got a long ride ahead of you there, Hogan. You think it's worth it?'

'What, bringing in the fellow who leads the only band of outlaws still operating in these parts? Yes, I should just about say it is.'

'Does Granger know about your personal interest in the man?'

'Couldn't say what he knows or don't know. Told him as me and DuBois were young'uns together. There's no more to it than that. You think I should lay off anybody as I once knew? That wouldn't be the straight path, not by a long sight.'

Maddocks looked at his friend strangely and said, 'You're straight as they come, nobody could ever doubt it. Still and all, I wonder if there's more here than anybody guesses.'

'So long, Maddocks. I'll see you in a week or two, when I've laid hands on Beau DuBois.'

'Goodbye, Hogan. You take a care now.'

As he headed into the mountains, Tim Hogan wondered if he would have done better to take the railroad, instead of sticking to the open country like this. He had a professional reason for his mode of travel though and it was this. You learn a good deal more as you go along if you are talking to folk and observing their faces the while. You might whizz by real fast on a railroad train, but you don't get a feel for the lie of the land, nor yet what people there are thinking and saying. Sure, he could have jumped on a train and arrived in Shelby, where DuBois' wife lived, in a matter of hours. Daresay, he thought to himself, that's what Granger would have done, but then Marshal Granger was a lousy lawman. He and Maddocks both knew it and he was sure that Maddocks would have done as he was doing, taking his time on horseback.

Little did he know it, but Hogan's path took him within five miles of DuBois' smallholding, where the man he was hunting was currently engaged in tidying up the place and preparing for his trip to the baths at Eureka Springs. Asking any number of questions around there would not have aided Tim Hogan in tracking down his man; there was not one person in that part of the state who had the slightest inkling that Beau DuBois and Frank Butler were really one and the same person.

So Hogan kept riding on east, hoping to reach Shelby in three or four days. It wasn't yet too cold for him to be sleeping out and so he could just keep going at whatever pace best suited him. His only concern was not pushing the mare too hard and making sure that her needs were tended to as well as could be.

Three days after Hogan had passed through the neighbourhood, the man known to everybody as Frank Butler packed a trunk and arranged for it to be delivered on to Eureka Springs. He intended to spend at least two weeks there. After that, he also packed a smaller bag for himself, with his shaving tackle, spare shirt and one or two other things to keep him going until his trunk arrived. Then he set off for Eureka Springs. Like Tim Hogan, he far preferred to ride than travel by railroad.

3

'Another glass of mineral water, Mr Butler?' The uniformed attendant stood respectfully at DuBois' elbow, with a carafe of the disgusting and sulphurous liquid, which was such an integral part of taking the cure, balanced on a silver tray.

'Why not?' answered DuBois. 'Live dangerously, I always say. You sure I can't have it mixed in with a little bourbon?'

'Ah now, Mr Butler,' said the man, smiling. 'You know our rules about strong liquor.'

Gerard DuBois had had over a week to learn the strict rules governing the clinic at which he had booked in for a fortnight. No alcohol, no meat, regular warm baths in the water which issued forth from the mountainside and, worst of all, nothing to drink, other than that same mineral water.

Irksome as the rules of the Eureka Springs Spa Hotel were, DuBois felt better than he had done in many months. Despite the increasingly chilly weather as November drew on, he had barely had a twinge of his rheumatic pains for the last few days. The treatment was certainly proving efficacious in his case.

Some called Eureka Springs Little Switzerland, due to its sanatoria and mountain air; for others, it was known as the city of steps. The town clung to the side of a mountain, the streets following the contours of the slopes. Pedestrians desirous of getting about the place in a hurry, were able to flit from street to street along a network of steps. It was tiring, walking up and down the side of a mountain in that way, just to reach your hotel, but the exercise too was good for those taking the waters. DuBois felt like a new man already.

There was little enough to do in the

town. It was the most genteel and respectable place that Gerard DuBois could ever recollect being in. Visitors from England had remarked that Eureka Springs wasn't like being in America at all; the atmosphere was more like that of a quiet, English spa town like Harrogate or Droitwich. Most of those staying here were invalids or, at the least, men and women like DuBois who hoped to recover their health after two or three weeks under the strict regime recommended by the doctors there.

The attendants at the Spa Hotel, where he was staying, all wore neat, navy blue uniforms. They gave the place the appearance, at least to DuBois eyes, of a private lunatic asylum. Although he had lately been thinking of himself as getting on a bit, especially as his forty-sixth birthday approached, DuBois found to his amazement that he was among the youngest of those staying in the hotel and taking the cure. This discovery had the effect of making him feel

young and boyish and putting something of a spring in his step. Yes, the stay
here had done him a power of good and
no mistake!

★ ★ ★

'You sure this'll be all right?' asked the
old mail clerk, doubtfully.

'You seed my badge,' Hogan told him.
'I'm a federal peace officer in pursuit of
a suspect. Law says as I can take any
steps necessary for to apprehend the
man and one o' those steps is looking at
them letters.'

This was, of course, a travesty of the
legal position, which would have required
a duly authorized and properly sworn-
out warrant to intercept the federal mail.
Tim Hogan was in a hurry though, and
didn't wish to alert anybody to the direction that his inquires were tending. So
he thought that a little bluff might do
the trick instead.

'Say,' said the clerk, in his quavering
and nervous voice, 'will you give me a

45

chit, signed with your name and badge number, so's I can later explain to my superviser if'n he asks any questions of me?'

'Tell you what,' responded Tim Hogan in a friendly and good natured tone of voice, 'I can do even better than that.'

The old man's face brightened and he said, 'You will?'

'Sure. If you don't let me look at the addresses on those letters, or if you obstruct me in anywise whatsoever, I'll arrest you right now for interfering with a federal marshal in the execution of his duty. Then I'll take you off and see you lodged in the federal prison at Little Rock. How does that suit you, old timer?'

'Land sakes,' said the clerk, 'there's no need to start issuing threats. Here, you help yourself.' He thrust a handful of letters at Hogan and then stomped off in a huff to the other end of the office.

Pauline DuBois had left three letters

at the office in the last week, all of which were due to be despatched that very day. What a mercy, thought Hogan to himself, that he had arrived in Shelby that morning.

Two of the letters could be ignored. One was to Mr Albert T. Booker. Since Pauline DuBois' maiden name was Booker, it was a fair guess that this was for a relative; maybe her father or brother. A second letter was addressed to an attorney in Little Rock. Which left the last one. This was to a Mr Frank Butler, care of the general store in a little hamlet through which Hogan had passed on his way to Shelby. He made a note of the address and then gave the letters back to the mail clerk, saying as he did so, 'Just you make sure as you don't tell a living soul that anybody was asking about this, you hear what I tell you?'

The old man looked hard at Tim Hogan and said, 'You sure you're a deputy marshal? You talk more like you're a badman.'

'You think I can catch ahold of some of those fellows without being a mite tougher than they are?' asked Hogan rhetorically, before leaving the office.

The ride back, along the road to Fayetteville, saw Tim Hogan in a far more cheerful mood than when he had been heading east. His hunch had paid off and he now had a name to work on. More than that, he had a definite, fixed geographical location in which to hunt. Things were looking up.

Something less than a week after leaving Shelby, Deputy Marshal Hogan was riding at a walking pace down a little lane that led between two fields. In the distance, the Ozarks could be seen, remote and clear. He had asked a few people in the neighbourhood about Frank Butler and garnered enough of a description to convince him that this was indeed the name under which Gerard DuBois was going, round here. This was promising, but he had now come to a dead end: nobody currently had any idea where Butler was. It was very frustrating. While he was brooding about this, Hogan turned a bend and found his path blocked by a buggy. It was being driven by a most attractive young woman, who appeared to be having some difficulty controlling the horse.

Hogan swept off his hat and said, 'Good day to you, ma'am. Do you need any help there?'

'Oh, I'm sorry to stop up the lane in this way. It's this creature. He just won't do as I require.'

'Let me get down and see if there's anything I can do.'

The deputy dismounted and went over to examine the horse and buggy. He said, 'Why, the harness is all twisted round here. The buckle's sticking in his hide like a cockle burr; no wonder he's cutting up rough!'

'Oh, could you fix it for me? I knew something was wrong.'

Hogan adjusted the straps of the harness and tightened one. The horse at once looked more comfortable and at ease. The girl said, 'I don't know how to thank you.'

'Well, you might favour me some information I am seeking. That is, if I really have earned your gratitude.'

'Oh, you surely have! What is it you want to know?'

'Well now, I'm looking for an old friend of mine. Fellow by the name of Frank Butler.'

'You're a friend of Mr Butler's? Why, I never met any such before. Are you in banking or something?'

'Banking? No, why would you think so?'

'Because,' said the girl innocently, 'Mr Butler said that his business was finance.'

Endeavouring to preserve his countenance, Tim Hogan said gravely, 'No, I'm in a different line of work, Miss . . . ?'

'Archer. Jane Archer. Are you really an old friend of Mr Butler's?'

'I am that. We used to play together as children. Got up to all kinds of scrapes when we was young'uns.'

'What a pity you've missed him.'

Hogan felt a sinking feeling in his heart. So close and now to have lost the trail. He said, 'Missed him, Miss Archer? How so? Don't he live round here any longer?'

'Oh yes, his place is over yonder,' said the girl, gesturing vaguely with her hand. 'Thing is though, he ain't there right now. He's gone away for a spell.'

Keeping his voice as casual and easy as could be, Hogan asked, 'You wouldn't happen to know, I suppose, where he's gone?'

'Lord, that's no mystery. He's taking the waters up in Eureka Springs. You know where that is?'

'Sure I do. Miss Archer, I am greatly obliged to you. If I have helped you, then you repaid me a heap. Thanks.'

Saying which, Tim Hogan touched up his horse and set off at a smart trot along the road which would eventually lead him to the town of Eureka Springs.

★ ★ ★

After the full two weeks, DuBois was just about ready to dig up and leave Eureka Springs. It was true that he felt fitter and healthier than he had for some years, but at the same time this must be the deadliest dull spot on the face of God's Earth. There was just *nothing* doing in the town. Although he had agreed to abide by the rules which stipulated that he should imbibe no intoxicating liquor during his stay at the Spa Hotel, nobody had said anything about card games. DuBois had prowled the streets, hopping nimbly up the steps from place to place. Incredible to relate, he could not discover a single game of poker being played in the whole of Eureka Springs. He had never heard of a such a thing in a town!

So it was that on a Friday night at about 8.30, Gerard DuBois was slumped in a chair in the lounge of the hotel, reading a New York paper which was a week out of date. Even so, there was enough to keep his interest; he had not been to New York for some years. So engrossed was he in the paper, that when somebody approached from behind with soft steps and then stood at his elbow, he said without looking up, 'No, thank you. I don't reckon I'll have any more of that noxious liquid you call mineral water.'

'Just as well,' said a voice which sounded strangely familiar. DuBois looked up, wondering if one of his men had tracked him here for some reason and found himself looking straight into the eyes of his childhood companion. He had barely had time to exclaim, 'Well, I'll be . . . ' when Hogan had drawn his pistol and then reached swiftly down to relieve DuBois of his own weapon.

'It's been a long time, DuBois,' said the Deputy.

'Lord, you might say so,' said DuBois, seemingly not at all put out by the turn of events. 'Why, we have not spoke face to face since, what, sixty-four? Leastways, at least twenty-five, twenty-six years.'

'It could be so,' said Hogan indifferently. 'I reckon there's no need for me to explain the play?'

'No, not at all. You're a lawman and you're arresting me. Mind telling me what for?'

'The bank in St Louis. Maybe the jewellery store as well.'

'Ah Hogan, who's putting the pressure on you to come this far to look for me? Some big guy in St Louis?'

'You talk too much, DuBois. You always did, even when you was a boy. Never you mind whose idea it was to come on your track. Here I am.'

DuBois stretched his arms above his head and then made to stand up. Hogan stepped back away and looked as though he had taken first pull on the trigger. 'Hell's afire, Hogan,' said the outlaw, 'I'm not going to start a fight here. Folk are staring enough as it is.'

Hogan looked round the lounge. It was true. Every eye was fixed upon them. He looked at the man sitting in the comfortable armchair and said, 'You going to give me any trouble? Will you try and escape?'

'No, not a bit of it. You caught me fair and square and I'll go with you now. Where you based?'

'Jacob's Lot. You know it?'

'Sure, nice little town. Tell you what, I'll engage to go with you to Jacob's Lot without trying to escape or aught of that kind. After that, we'll see.'

Tim Hogan stared searchingly for a second or two at his childhood friend. Then he nodded his head briefly and said, 'That's good enough for me.' He put his own gun back in its holster and tucked DuBois' pistol in his belt. 'Come on,' he said, 'let's go to your room and collect some of your things.'

Those watching this scene were unsure whether they had seen a couple of friends fooling around or something else entirely. At first, it had looked like there might be trouble brewing, but then when that nice Mr Butler went off, practically arm in arm with the other fellow, they figured that there couldn't have been anything to worry about.

To anybody unfamiliar with the sense of honour which was so precious to many men at that time, it will perhaps seem scarcely credible that Hogan should have behaved as he did. On receiving DuBois' word that he would not try to make a run for it, the deputy marshal simply holstered his gun and gave the matter no more thought. The two of them had fought together for the Confederacy and both were ardent adherents of the Rattlesnake Code. It is entirely likely that both men would sooner have hazarded their lives than risk breaking an oath. DuBois had given his parole and promised to come along to Jacob's Lot and as far as Deputy Marshal Hogan was concerned, that was the end of the matter.

The two men walked up the grand staircase which led to the bedrooms. Hogan indicated the red carpet and said, 'Looks like a damned whorehouse. How come you fetched up in a place like this? I thought your tastes ran to a simpler life.'

'I got the rheumatism. This seemed the best spot to come and tackle it.'

'Ah,' said Hogan, 'that explains a deal. You're getting past it, DuBois. I reckon as a nice, warm cell somewhere will keep you out of all those draughts and dampness. We'll have your pains eased in next to no time.'

When they reached the room, Hogan was astonished at the amount of clothing and other belongings. He said, 'Time was when you used to travel lighter than this.'

'Is it all right with you if I pack up the trunk and get the hotel to send it on to my home?'

'Which home would that be? The one where your wife and son live or that other place, nearer to here?'

'Does it matter overmuch?'

'I guess not. Let me see what you're putting in there, mind. For aught I know to the contrary, you'll be filling it with stolen jewellery.'

At this, DuBois laughed out loud. He said, 'How'd you find being a lawman? Does it suit you?'

'It suits well enough. I ain't fitted out to do much else, so it's good that I like the job.'

As he folded his clothes neatly and stowed them in the trunk, DuBois said, 'I passed you in the street a while back, you know. Somebody pointed you out to me. I would have known you in any case.'

'Can't say the same to you, I'm afeared. Chief thing I recollect 'bout your appearance was all those black curls. They seem to have faded somewhat.'

Running his hand ruefully over his greying hair, DuBois said, 'Ain't that the truth!'

The two men sauntered casually down the stairs to the reception, where Tim Hogan stood discreetly at a distance while DuBois settled his bill and made arrangements for his trunk to be sent on. After he had conducted this business, DuBois rejoined the deputy and said, 'I'd offer you a drink, for old times' sake, but this place is dry. We could go down the street a pace though, if you want a whiskey to wash the dust from your mouth. You look like you been doing a lot of travelling lately.'

'All the way from Jacob's Lot to Shelby and then back here again,' said Hogan. 'But it wouldn't feel right to stand at the bar with you. This is business, not pleasure.'

'You can sometimes combine the two,' suggested the other. 'Does no harm to anybody.'

'Let's just get started back to Jacob's Lot.'

'As you will. It's your show.'

DuBois' horse was down at the livery stable, right at the foot of the mountain. Hogan's, on the other hand was hitched right outside the hotel. This was irritating for DuBois, because he could have just walked down the steps, avoiding all the winding streets which looped back and forth down the side of the mountain. Howsoever, he felt that

59

he really ought to walk along with his old friend and since there was no question of taking a horse down all those flights of steps, it meant DuBois walking a good long way beside the deputy marshal.

'You want that I should walk ahead of you, Tim, so that you can see where I am?'

'Don't be a damned fool,' said Hogan. 'You given me your oath. I ain't a-goin' to watch you every second. You want to break your word, it's you as'd be the loser, not me. I'd lose a prisoner, but you'd sacrifice your honour.'

'Just checking,' DuBois said. 'Anyways, it will give us the chance to catch up a little. You never marry?'

The two of them walked down at a leisurely pace, looking for all the world like old friends. Hogan didn't at first answer the question, but after a space he said, 'I never found it easy to get along with women. You remember that. Never could rightly understand them. No, I ain't married. I gather as you left it late in the day, yourself?'

'You might well say so,' said DuBois, laughing. 'I was nigh on forty when I finally made it to the altar.'

'You don't think as it would have been better for your bride, had you stayed at home a little more?'

'Ah, yes. Yes, that may well be so. You know what it's like. You pick up a taste for some things. In my case, it was getting money without working for it.'

Tim Hogan didn't say anything further until they were at the foot of the slopes and near the livery stable where DuBois' horse was. Then he said, 'You know, it strikes me as you always had a sight too much money which you didn't have to work for. I should say as your childhood set you on that path, expecting money for nothing, I mean.'

The owner of the livery stable greeted DuBois affably. 'Why, good evening Mr Butler. Don't tell me you're leaving us?'

'Duty calls George, duty calls. My friend here has a sure-fire proposition for me that I can't turn down.'

61

'Is he a speculator too?' asked the man.

At this point, Tim Hogan cut in, not wishing to see himself made the butt of DuBois' jokes. He said, 'No, I ain't what you would term a speculator. I'm a fellow who only goes for dead certs. This here is one that me and Mr Butler are embarked upon now. Wouldn't you say so, Butler?'

'Happen you have a point, Mr Hogan,' said DuBois gravely. 'You may well have a good point.'

After his horse was tacked up and ready to go, DuBois settled his bill and there was no further hinderance for the two of them to set out for Jacob's Lot. The weather was getting chillier by the day and he had some trepidation about the passage through the mountains; wondering if the cold would set off his rheumatics again. Whether or no, there was little enough that he could do about it. He was, as you might say, bound to the side of Tim Hogan, at least until they reached his office. That

was as far as he had pledged his word
and after they got there, then they
would just have to see what chanced.

4

The air up in the Ozarks was bitingly fresh and clear. Another couple of weeks and they might expect to see the first flakes of snow up in the mountains, but with luck, thought Hogan, they would be through them in no more than three or four days.

Anybody watching the two men ride along, side by side, would have taken them at once for old acquaintances. They looked as relaxed and casual as you like. 'Remember when we fought at Shiloh?' said DuBois, out of the blue. 'Hoo, that was hot fighting.'

'I recall,' said Tim Hogan. ' 'Member it like it was but yesterday.'

'Didn't even know you were there that day. Leastways, not during the battle itself, you understand. Wasn't until after it was all over, when I came across you in that tent. You recollect that? That was a wound you had.'

'Minie ball clean through my thigh,' said Hogan. 'Still pains me in the cold weather. I bled like a stuck hog, thought it was all up with me.'

'That's a while back, now.'

'Best part of thirty years. Spring of sixty-two, not long after the war started.'

'Was it though?' said DuBois. 'Yes, I think perhaps you are right. We were eighteen.'

They camped out that night in the woods. It was cold and because they were not looking to encounter any trouble, they lit a cheerful fire, which painted the nearby tree trunks a warm, ruddy colour. They didn't have much in the way of food, but Tim Hogan had enough coffee for them to brew up and they made do with that and a couple of stale rolls that he also had in his pack.

The two men lounged at their ease by the fire drinking their coffee. Both of them lit their pipes.

'You know what?' said DuBois. 'This

is like being back in the army again. Short commons, uncomfortable place to sleep and just an old friend for company.'

This made Hogan feel uncomfortable and he said, 'It's only a job for me, you know. Bringing you in, that's to say. It ain't what you might call personal.'

DuBois looked at his old friend quizzically and smiled. Then he said coarsely, 'That's a heap of horseshit and we both know it to be so. Those big shots in St Louis didn't set you to go chasing over to my wife in Shelby.'

'I was acting under instructions,' said Hogan flatly. 'No more to the case than that.'

'No you weren't. Maybe at first, I'll grant you that, when you and your posse came up here into the mountains hunting for us. Then you lost us and the trail went cold.'

'How'd you know 'bout that?'

'Saw you,' said DuBois cheerfully. 'Saw you and, what's more, saved your life, did you but know it.' He related the story of the man at his side who would have shot down the deputy marshal without issuing a challenge.

'Well, I'm mighty obliged to you for that,' said Hogan, when once he had digested this astonishing intelligence. 'I'd no idea that I'd even been spotted.'

'You were like a damned bloodhound. I knew you would o' found us in the end. What happened, the rest of your men wanted to cut for home?'

'Somethin' o' the sort.'

'I never could abide seeing the rattlesnake code broken, you know. Shooting a man in the back like that, without giving him a chance to defend himself. It wouldn't have happened back when we were boys.'

'Times change.'

There was silence for a while and then DuBois said, 'You still haven't told me why you came out looking for me especially. Come on Tim, it's the least you can do.'

It came as somewhat of a shock to Hogan, hearing his Christian name spoken like that by a man he had nursed such grudges against for better than two decades now. But still and all, DuBois was in the right; he did owe him some slight explanation.

'My ma, she used t'take in washing, you know,' said Hogan. 'We was that poor, that even with pa out working all the hours God sent, she still had to wash out other folk's clothes for 'em. Just so us young'uns had enough to eat.'

'Hell, I knew that,' said DuBois carelessly. 'That didn't signify. Least-ways, not to me.'

'You say so now. You forgotten how you'd give me money? Couple o' dimes here, a nickel there? Like I was a charity case or something? You forget that?'

'So? I shared my allowance with you. What of it? We were friends.'

'You say you never looked down on me, on account of how poor my folks was?'

'Look down on you?' asked DuBois, clearly dumbfounded at this accusation.

'Why, whatever can you mean?'

'On account of we lived in that little cabin of course, while your father was the biggest plantation owner in the county.'

DuBois shook his head in amazement and then laughed out loud. He said, 'You couldn't have got it more wrong, had you set out and tried for to do it! Look down on you? Why man, I envied you!'

Now it was Tim Hogan's turn to look staggered. 'Envied me? Why the hell would you do that? Ah, I should o' known. You're mockin' me.'

'Not at all, man. You had everything I wanted. My mother was a Creole, you know. She dug up and left when I was a baby. I hardly saw my father. I was raised by the black folks, you know, my Mammy and the other servants. I only saw my father for five minutes in the evening. Those times I came by your place were the happiest days I recall in my whole, entire childhood.'

Deputy Marshal Hogan said nothing

at all after this for perhaps five minutes. Then he announced abruptly, 'I guess I had the case reckoned up all wrong. Happen I owe you an apology.'

'It's nothing. It was all a long time since.'

'It's why I came a-huntin' of you.'

Suddenly, Gerard DuBois began laughing helplessly.

'What's the joke?' asked Hogan gruffly.

'We been over thirty years at cross purposes, is all,' said DuBois. 'You don't find that funny?'

'Not overmuch. It's like to cost you ten years in gaol.'

'Ah hell, let's see what happens.'

* * *

When deputy Tim Hogan walked into the office at Jacob's Lot with his prisoner, it created a sensation. In the first place, he was bringing in one of the most famous outlaws still operating in that part of the country and not only that, this desperado was strolling along next to his supposed captor in the most amiable fashion one could hope to see. If you didn't know better, you might have thought that they were old friends taking the air.

Marshal Granger was more than a mite taken aback when his deputy walked in with Beau DuBois. He hadn't really believed for a moment that Hogan would be able to track down the fellow, never mind be able to bring him in. The prisoner was sporting no handcuffs nor chains, wasn't hogtied and thrown over a horse or anything; just walking into the marshal's office like he was entering a store or something. Had he but known it, Granger's mouth was hanging open at the sight and his jaw moving aimlessly, giving him more than passing resemblance to a landed fish. Then he collected himself and sprang into action.

'Hogan, have you lost your mind?' cried Marshal Granger. 'You let that there villain walk down the road like that, so's he can break loose at any which time he want? Lord God, I never saw the like!'

71

'He gave me his word,' said Tim Hogan, as though that was the end of the matter.

'You and me goin' to have to talk about this some,' said Granger, standing up, drawing his gun and pointing it in the general direction of DuBois. 'You fella, you best just walk nice and easy into the back here, with me. I want you under lock and key.'

Before obeying this curt instruction, the outlaw turned to Hogan and said, 'I'm glad we got that other business cleared up, you know.' He extended his hand to the deputy, who took it. The two of them shook warmly, which proceeding was eyed with disfavour by Granger.

After he had escorted the dangerous criminal to the little barred section in the back room of the office, Marshal Granger came back and said to Hogan, 'I don't know what it is with you and that man.'

Hogan shrugged and said, 'What's it matter? I said I'd bring him in and here he is. I don't see as you've aught to complain of.'

'Do you not?' exclaimed Granger. 'Like I say, we needs must have a little conversation on this, but not now.'

As he walked back to his little house on the edge of town, Tim Hogan turned over the events of the last week or so and found that it was as if a weight had been lifted from him. For nigh on the whole of his adult life, he had laboured under the sense of shame which he had felt about his humble origins. The larger part of this shame had been caused by having a close friend who was so much higher up the social scale than he; the sense of being looked down upon had been eating away at him like a canker, ever since. To learn that it had all been a creation of his imagination was surely a good feeling. The only bad part of it was that this resolution had been reached at the expense of his childhood friend's liberty. That, at least, was how he saw the case when he went to bed that night.

At six the next morning, Hogan was awakened from his slumbers by a furious banging at his door. The drumming and kicking did not stop and the person without continued with unabated vigour. As he pulled on his trousers and made his way down the stairs, it seemed to Hogan that the banging was reaching a crescendo. He would have something sharp to say to whoever was knocking on his door fit to rouse the entire neighbourhood.

When Hogan opened the front door, Marshal Granger burst in, without so much as a by-your-leave. His first words were not at all encouraging. He said, 'Hogan, you are in the deepest shit I ever heard tell of. You're on the right path to end up in the penitentiary yourself.'

'What are you talking about?' asked Hogan, and then recollected himself enough to add, 'Sir.'

'What am I talking about? I'm talking about that great friend of yours as you brought in yesterday. You remember him, surely? Pair of you came ambling into the office like brothers and then, before you left, you shook hands with the fellow. Remember that?'

'I recall it. Then what?'

'Then what? Then this. Your friend has bust out of his cell and killed Tyler Maddocks in the process. He's on the loose now and if you don't fetch him back here, I'm going to bust you out of being a deputy and then kick your arse all the way to the gaol. It's bad enough that Maddocks is dead, but on top of that, I already wired St Louis and told them as we had DuBois. Now I got to contact 'em again and tell 'em I lost him. What sort of fool am I going to look?'

After he had been lodged in the tiny holding cell at the back of the marshal's office, Gerard DuBois had sat on the bunk and considered carefully the options open to him. He had fulfilled his oath to Tim Hogan. In exchange for not being brought in cuffed or tied up, he had made no attempt to escape. As far as he could see, he was now free to try and escape, without compromising his honour. The thought of being shipped off to a federal penitentiary again for five or ten years, was not an attractive one. Why, he didn't see all that much of his son as it was. If he didn't take determined action, the boy would be all but grown up by the time DuBois was free again. No, it would not do at all.

If he was going to break out, then the sooner he did it the better. Once St Louis sent men down to collect him, then he could forget any chance of getting away. They would stick him in the city gaol, which had proper guards and high walls. No, there wasn't apt to be a better place to get out of than this one-horse, two-bit, hick-town's marshal's office.

After seeing DuBois safely locked up for the night, Marshal Granger had gone off to the saloon, to preen himself on his successful capture of the most dangerous man in three states. Already, he was editing and adapting the story of Beau DuBois' arrest; reducing Hogan's role in the affair to a minor part and showing how he, Brent Granger, had the necessary foresight to send one of his deputies off to bring the man in. He left Tyler Maddocks in charge of the office.

At a little after two that night, an hour or so after Granger had drunk himself into a stupor and when Tim Hogan had been asleep for some four hours, Maddocks was sitting at the desk in the front of the office, catching up on some paperwork. He heard a loud crash, followed by a groan. The deputy was on his feet in a moment and walked briskly into the back room, to find DuBois laying on his back on the floor of the little cell. The man's eyes were closed and he didn't look to be breathing.

'Hey, DuBois!' said Tyler Maddocks roughly. 'What the devil are you playing at?' There was no answer from the man on the floor, who remained utterly still.

Could he have taken poison or something? thought Maddocks. Out loud, he said, 'You better not be screwing me around, DuBois. I mean it now, if you're fooling, you best quit now. You hear what I'm tellin' you?' There was still no sign of life. The deputy was beginning to be seriously alarmed. He went back into the front part of the office and took the key down from where it hung on the wall above the desk.

The cell in which Gerard DuBois was being held was really no more than a half a small room, which had been isolated by means of installing stout iron bars, which stretched from ceiling to floor. A barred metal door provided access to the cell, which contained a single bunk bed and a chamber pot. There was nothing in the confined space which could possibly be used as a weapon and the prisoner had been searched and all his belongings removed before being locked up. That being so, Maddocks felt that it was fairly safe to unlock the door and see what was ailing the man who lay on the floor. He loosened his pistol in its holster first and made sure that once he had opened the door, his right hand was hovering above the hilts of the weapon; ready, at the first sign of trouble, to draw.

There was still no sign of life from DuBois. He just lay there on his back, his arms stretched up above his head at an awkward angle. The deputy prodded him with his toe and said, 'Come on man, get up now.' There was no response. Beginning to be seriously concerned now, Tyler Maddocks bent down and peered into the prone man's eyes. There was no flickering of the eyelids and no sign either that the fellow was even breathing. He leaned closer, quite sure now that something was wrong. At that moment, DuBois' eyes opened and he said,

'Hidy!'

Before Maddocks had a chance to react, the prisoner had grasped the chamber pot which lay a foot or so from his head and brought it up, smashing it as hard as he could into the deputy's face. Maddocks dropped like a pole-axed ox. In one smooth, flowing, cat-like movement, Gerard DuBois was on his feet. The man who had entered the cell was breathing stertorously. DuBois reached down and unbuckled the gun-belt from the deputy's waist and strapped it on himself. Then, locking the cell door behind him, he went into the front office and began looking for a rifle. There was a walk-in closet, the key to which was on the same ring as that of the cell. This little cubby hole was lined with rifles and scatterguns. Ammunition in neat cardboard boxes was stacked on a shelf. He helped himself to a rifle and then took two boxes of shells; one for the forty-five at his hip and the other for the carbine. These he emptied into the pockets of his trousers. By the time DuBois walked out of the marshal's office, with a rifle tucked under his arm, a little over two minutes had elapsed since the moment that Tyler

Maddocks had entered the cell.

The next task to face DuBois was finding a horse. He didn't want to delay his departure from Jacob's Lot by fooling around with breaking into the livery stable and stealing a saddle, then blundering about in a dark field to get hold of a horse. Fortunately, this particular problem more or less solved itself. Although it lacked only a few minutes to two in the morning, there were still a few stray travellers on main street. One of these was an obviously intoxicated man on a horse which was proceeding at a leisurely walk, stopping at frequent intervals, its rider being too drunk to urge it onwards. DuBois sprinted towards this animal and unceremoniously dragged the rider off and dumped him in the road. Then he mounted swiftly and cantered down the street and out of town.

Four and a half hours after Gerard DuBois had effected his escape from the marshal's office in Jacob's Lot, Tim Hogan walked round the office, trying to figure out what had happened. While he was doing this, Marshal Granger alternately brooded and raged in the background, making it difficult for Hogan to think clearly.

One thing seemed to be clear and that was that Tyler Maddocks had unlocked the cell door and gone in alone. This in itself was strange and suggested that Maddocks must have thought that there was an emergency of some kind. Surely, if he did enter the cell, then Maddocks would have been alert to the possibility of danger from a man like DuBois? The only explanation must be that he thought DuBois to be helpless; either through sickness or injury.

There was a rifle missing from the armoury, along with a couple of boxes of ammunition. In addition to that, Tyler Maddocks' own gun-belt and pistol had been taken. Wherever he was now, there could be not the slightest doubt that Gerard DuBois was armed and dangerous.

According to the doctor, who was not best pleased to be roused from his bed at six in the morning, Maddocks' death was an unlucky chance. The blow from the china chamber pot had caught him right on the temple and he must have died within minutes. The intention had almost certainly been to stun the unfortunate deputy, rather than actually kill him. Nevertheless, causing the death of a deputy federal marshal in the course of escaping from custody was a hanging matter. It was unlikely that Marshal Granger would let St Louis have the fugitive now, if and when he was recaptured. There was a score to be settled right here in Jacob's Lot.

'Well,' said Marshal Granger impatiently, 'what are you going to do?'

'I guess it's pretty plain which way he'll be heading . . . ' began Hogan, only to have the marshal break in with the utmost irascibility.

'It may be plain to you Hogan, but happen you'd like to favour those of us as is a bit slower on the uptake with your views?'

'Well now, they opened up the Indian

Territories to settlers only last year. 'Fore that, it was regular bandit country out that way. Still is in a lot o' places. That's where DuBois's gone, for a bet. He can't go back to his wife and child, he knows that's the first place we'll come lookin'. He wants to hole up somewhere, wait 'til the heat dies down. Mark what I say, he'll be headin' for the territories.'

'What are you sitting round here for then, scratching your arse?' said Granger. 'Why ain't you out there, trying to track him down?'

'You want that I should make out my report first? I haven't yet wrote down all that happened on my way back from Shelby. I found out some right interestin' — '

At this point, Marshal Granger's meagre supply of patience ran out entirely and he bawled at the top of his voice, 'No, you blockhead, I don't want you to write anything at all down. I'm telling you to get out there and find that cowson and then bring him back here so that we can hang him.'

5

Although he didn't know that his escape from the marshal's office in Jacob's Lot was now a hanging matter, Gerard DuBois was even so quite anxious to put as much space between himself and that town as was humanly possible. Just as his childhood friend had predicted, he was indeed heading into what had, until the previous year, been the Indian Nations.

Unlike the cramped little areas which comprised the reservations, the huge, sprawling mass of land which made up the Indian Territories, home to the five so-called civilized tribes, was vast; at least as big as many states. Indeed, it was soon to become the state of Oklahoma. In 1889, in flat defiance of any number of previous treaties between Washington and the Indians, the Indian Nations had been opened up to settlement by white men. There had been a land rush and within a few years, it was plain that this would be civilized land, just like the rest of the country.

Two classes of person were mightily ticked off by the abolition of the Indian Territory. The Indians themselves were naturally less than enchanted to find that they no longer controlled their own land, but there were also quite a few white men who were in the habit of hiding out in the territories, reasonably free from the threat of arrest. Every so often, a posse would come looking for someone, but so immense was the area, that it was a hopeless task.

It was certain-sure that he could not head back to his wife in Shelby: that would be the very first place that folk would look for DuBois. Staying in Missouri was out of the question and so cutting across the state line into the newly settled lands that would soon become the state of Oklahoma seemed the only sensible dodge.

So swiftly had he made his departure from Jacob's Lot, that DuBois had not thought to search the marshal's office for any money. He had quite literally, not a cent to his name. That would need to be the first thing to be remedied, before he could even consider any long term plans.

For long distance travel, the railroad was the only means that most people would consider. The days of travelling by stage for hundreds of miles was long gone. However, for shorter journeys to out of the way places, where the railroad had not yet flung its tentacles, there were still a few stages running. One of these ran from Fayetteville in Arkansas down to Fort Smith in the territories. If DuBois' memory served him right, it ran each day and with a little luck, he should be able to intercept it, just where it entered the territories.

It had been two in the morning when he had broken out of that cell and DuBois had ridden the moon from the sky. The horse seemed to be lively enough, which was a mercy, and by branching off the road once the sun had come up, he hoped to elude any pursuers. Would that bastard marshal in Jacob's Lot rally a posse and come after him? It was possible, he supposed, but he didn't find it all that likely. Most of the men up for those tricks had already spent a week chasing him just lately and probably they would be reluctant to get drawn into another hunt of that sort so soon after the last one.

DuBois had no idea how soon after he lit out of Jacob's Lot, the pursuit would have begun. He gauged that he might have a four or five hours' start, which was pretty close to the truth. He felt that he could afford to rest up for an hour or so and give his horse the chance to graze a little and recover its strength. He did not know the time exactly, but calculated from the height of the sun in the sky, that it might be about ten. He should be able to take an hour's rest now and then still be on the Fayetteville Road by three, when the stage to Fort Smith was due to pass.

It took no great mental effort to guess that Tim Hogan would soon be riding out after him. DuBois really did not want to go up against his old friend, especially now that they had cleared up what had evidently been a long-running grudge. All he wanted now was to lay up for a space and then find a way of giving up this game for good. He had been brought up sharp by that short stay in the cell, combined with the prospect of spending the next five or ten years being locked up in that way. If he could get out of this now, then he was damned if would carry out any more robberies. Times were changing and the game wasn't worth the candle any more. As he lay there, DuBois wondered if that smallholding up by the foothills of the Ozarks could provide him and his family with a living. Then his heart sank, as he realized that Hogan knew all about that now. It would never be safe for him to go back to the place.

★   ★   ★

Tim Hogan was feeling pretty confused as he trotted out of Jacob's Lot that morning. A good deal of his bitterness against his old friend had evaporated. Even now, after the death of Tyler Maddocks, he did not really want to drag DuBois back here to hang. On the other hand, being a lawman was far too deeply ingrained in his character for him not to do his best to track down Gerard DuBois. He knew that his own future career depended upon fetching DuBois back from wherever he had run to and Hogan didn't think he had the heart now, when he was nearly fifty, to start in a completely new line of work. It was the devil of a thing, but he supposed that he would just have to do as he was bid.

One thing that was ultimately to have far-reaching consequences was that because of Granger's insistence that his deputy should set off at once in pursuit of Gerard DuBois, nobody other than Hogan knew about the little bolthole near Fayetteville. Not that either Tim

Hogan nor anybody else had even thought about this at that point.

Three miles out of town, as he was heading south west along the track, Hogan caught sight of a rider heading in his direction. He spurred on his horse to a gallop and when he had reached the man, reined in and blocked his way.

'What's to do?' said the man, looking a little put out to have his path obstructed in this way.

'I'm a deputy federal marshal,' said Hogan, affording the fellow a brief glimpse of the badge on his jacket. 'You seen anybody on this track this morning? Heading the same way as I am?'

The man appeared to think this question over carefully, before saying, 'There a reward in the case?'

'There's an arrest in the case, if you hinder me in my duty. How's that suit you?'

'No need to get scratchy,' said the man. 'Saw a man about three or four hours back. It was still pitch dark, and I couldn't make him out too good. Had the idea though that he was trying not to be seen.'

'That the best you can do?'

'I reckon so.'

'Thanks for your help.'

It wasn't much to go on, but perhaps it was better than nothing. Hogan knew in his heart that Gerard DuBois would be going into the territories. He urged the horse forward into a canter.

★ ★ ★

As the crow flies, Fayetteville is only about a hundred miles from Fort Smith. The road which twists and turns through the mountains between them, effectively doubles that distance when travelling by road. Now that the Indian Territories had been opened up though, there was a steady flow of people wanting to make that journey west from Arkansas. The sight of the bright red stagecoach was, by 1890, something of an anachronism. Gerard DuBois felt the absurdity of his situation as he sat on his horse, waiting for the stage to come down the road from the mountains and into the plain.

DuBois had started out as a road agent or highwayman after the end of the War between the States and he found it more than a little sad that twenty-five years later, he was once more reduced to robbing a coach just for the money which the passengers might have about their person. But there it was; needs must, when the devil drives. He would need the wherewithal for food and drink and this looked to him to be the quickest way of getting hold of a little cash money.

There was a brief flash of scarlet up in the drab-coloured hills. DuBois turned his horse, so that its rump was facing the oncoming stage, and pulled his neckerchief up and secured it over the lower half of his face. There now, he thought to himself, I must look the part now. I can't see any stagecoach driver arguing the point with me, especially when once he finds that he's looking down the barrel of my gun. Now he could hear the distant thundering of the horses' hoofs as the team of four headed towards him. Why, he thought, this is quite like the old days. Just me and my own wits to depend upon. He had been so used in recent years to working with a gang, that he had all but forgotten that peculiar thrill of undertaking an action such as this, without a body to help him.

Would the driver of the stage find it a mite odd that a lone rider was sitting near the road, with his back to the oncoming vehicle? If so, then he gave no sign of it, because there was no diminution in the sound of the hoofs, nor the rattle of the wheels, which DuBois could also hear now. It was time to act. He whirled his horse round and then spurred it on towards the stagecoach, cocking his rifle and bringing it up as he did so.

Gerard DuBois need not have had any apprehension about the effect that his appearance might have upon the driver of the stage. The man reined in his horses at once and, as soon as they came to a halt, he threw up his hands in token of his desire not to get shot. As DuBois drew near, the driver cried, 'Don't shoot. I ain't offering any resistance!'

A woman's head emerged briefly from a side window, but was rapidly withdrawn as soon as she caught sight of the masked rider. As he came close, DuBois said to the driver, 'No need to be affeared. If you all do just as I say, there'll be nobody hurt.' He spoke gruffly and tried to make his voice sound little less educated than usual. He continued, 'Just throw down that scattergun I see by your foot.'

The driver picked up the sawn-off scattergun and pitched it to one side. Once he had done so, DuBois walked his horse forward to the side of the stage and said loudly, 'All you folk in there, I'm not a going to hurt you. All I'm after is cash money, not jewellery, watches or aught like that.'

At once the woman he had seen

poking her head out of the window before, repeated the performance. She must have been about thirty years of age and was exceedingly beautiful. She had an olive complexion and lustrous, blue-black hair piled up on the top of head. DuBois figured that she might be Spanish or Mexican.

'You're a rare scoundrel,' said the woman, her husky voice bearing the faintest trace of an accent, 'waylaying innocent travellers in this way. Are you not ashamed?'

'Well ma'am,' said DuBois, a little sheepishly, 'I kind of have my tail in a crack at this present moment, or I wouldn't be about this game.'

'I suppose you want my money as well?' said the woman.

'Not just yours, ma'am. I want all the money being carried by you and the rest of the passengers.' DuBois glanced anxiously around. Every second's delay in robberies of this sort, increased the likelihood of some stray rider fetching up and involving himself in the affair.

He said, 'I'd be mighty obliged if you'd all just hurry up about it, too.'

'Very well,' said the woman, 'let me take it from my purse.' Looking back later, DuBois decided that this marked the point at which he knew that he was getting too old for adventures of this sort. Twenty years ago, he would have had some inkling that things were about to go wrong. The Spanish looking woman, opened the little purse and then reached out her hand to DuBois. Automatically, he moved forward and stretched out his own hand; whereupon she shot him with the little muff pistol concealed in her palm. He felt a searing and agonising pain in his left upper arm, near the shoulder. Then he heard a sharp click, indicating that the woman had fired the second barrel of the pistol, but that the cartridge had misfired.

Before the echo from the shot had fully died away, DuBois was aware from the corner of his eye, that the driver was getting down from his perch; presumably in order to retrieve his scattergun.

There was no telling if any of the other passengers were carrying weapons and so DuBois did the only sensible thing he could do under the circumstances. He bolted.

Shortly after he galloped off, DuBois heard the rolling boom of the scatter-gun, which he supposed had been discharged in his direction. He had put sufficient distance between himself and the stagecoach to ensure that he was in no danger by then, but it was still a humiliating end to the exploit. That driver must have been sixty, if he was a day! He, Beau DuBois, had been defeated by a woman and an old man! When a thing like that happens, it surely is time to be thinking about another line of work.

It didn't seem wise to halt until he was well clear of the stage. When he did so, DuBois discovered to his alarm that he was bleeding heavily. The bullet from the Derringer, or whatever the hell that wretched woman had had hidden in her hand, had torn through the muscles of his upper arm and probably nicked a vein in the process. At least, he hoped and prayed that it was a vein. If an artery had been torn open, then he was as good as dead, right now.

He found that he was breathing rapidly with both the excitement of the incident and also the exertion of the galloping. DuBois knew that this tended to make blood flow more quickly and so he made a deliberate effort to slow down his breathing and give his heart a chance to stop racing. The sleeve of his jacket was sodden with blood, which was also dripping from his fingertips. The best thing would be to raise the arm above his head and keep still for an hour or two. Only thing was, DuBois knew that he did not have an hour to waste on such foolishness. For all he knew to the contrary, a posse from Jacob's Lot would come into sight at any second and then drag him back into captivity. Well, not while he had breath in his body they wouldn't. He might be down, but he certainly wasn't out yet!

★　★　★

Tim Hogan was making slow but steady progress into the newly settled territories. He hadn't been down this way for a while and could see how it was changing swiftly. Homesteaders were moving on to the empty land, covering it with a patchwork quilt of little fields. Give it ten, twenty years at the most, and this would be just another part of the non-Indian country. Both he and the man he was chasing would be out of place in such a land. The days of the outlaw were numbered, but so were those of the lone deputy in pursuit of his quarry. The two of them were relics from an earlier and wilder age.

From time to time, Hogan would hail some man working in a field, or a woman washing clothes by the side of a stream and ask if they had seen hide or hair of the man he was trying to run to ground. Nobody had seen anybody and even if they had, their concerns were more immediate and practical than helping him find some bandit or other.

The homesteads were clustered together, with wide expanses of empty land between them. It was while Hogan was riding through one of these largely deserted areas that he had a most unnerving encounter. He was not really sticking to the track, because he doubted if the man he was following was doing so. It was only when you thought and behaved like a fugitive, that you had any real chance of catching your man. So it was that as he trotted along a ridge of high ground which overlooked the road to Fort Smith, Hogan saw three strange figures ahead of him. They were all on foot and at first, he could not be sure if they were even humans. They could have been three lumbering bears when seen from five hundred yards away.

He had no special reason for investigating the figures ahead of him, but they were moving in the same general direction in which he was travelling and so Hogan saw no need to alter his course. As he drew closer, he realized that they were definitely human and not animal. All three were covered in thick furs, either buffalo or bearskin; he couldn't be sure until he got right up close. The bare skin, including their hands and faces, were smeared and bedaubed with what looked like a mixture of paint, mud and clay. No wonder he hadn't been able to see at first glance that they were men!

The men took no notice at all of Hogan. He pulled up and waited for them to walk past him. From the fact that they had feathers, as well as mud, stuck to their bodies, he figured that they were probably Indians, but he had no idea what tribe they might belong to. They trudged forward as though in a trance. All three were carrying not guns but bows and lithe, springy-looking lances. Hogan had never seen Indians tricked out like this in his life and eyed them cautiously, wondering what they were about. It was as well that he did so, because no sooner had the three of them passed him, than one whirled round and hurled his lance straight at Hogan. Because he had been watching them so closely, Hogan managed to move in time, so that the vicious looking weapon sailed past him. Then, all three of the weird and outlandishly decorated men ran at him.

It was instinct which made Tim Hogan dig his spurs hard into the horse's flanks, which carried him out of harm's way. He fully expected to hear a shot and perhaps feel the jarring impact of a ball in his back, but there was nothing of the kind. When he looked back, it was to see that the three Indians had carried on in the same direction and were apparently taking no further notice of him. 'That's right odd!' he muttered to himself.

You could see where some of the Indians hereabouts might be more than a little ticked off about having their land invaded and settled by a heap of white men. That was all quite under-standable. What was strange was that they hadn't shot him. He couldn't recollect when last he saw one of those lances or spears being used like that. Surely they had at least one gun among the three of them? Not that he wasn't grateful that they had not, but still. Men on foot attacking an armed rider; that was funny as well. It was plain that there was something in the wind, some missing factor of which he was unaware. Hogan was glad in a way that the little incident had occurred. It had tipped him the wink that there was trouble afoot and he knew that he would have to take a little more care from now on.

★ ★ ★

Ahead, DuBois saw a little house, what they used to call a soddie when he was young. It had been built from turfs cut from the ground and piled into walls. The roof was made of the same material and from the tin chimney stack, a thin plume of black smoke trickled up into the sky. It was taking the hell of a risk, but he truly didn't see that he had another choice: not the way he was currently fixed. The bleeding didn't show any signs of slowing down and if he didn't stop soon and rest up, he would be fainting from blood loss.

Although he had taken more than one bullet in him in the past, DuBois was beginning to be frightened. Somehow, when you had your men around you, everything was made easier and less alarming. He had, over the last few miles of his journey since attempting to rob the stage, come to the realization that he was afraid of dying. He had never set much store by death in the past, but now it was riding alongside him, he was scared all right.

There was the chance that whoever lived here would either refuse to help him or send word to the law, but what else was there for him to do? DuBois slithered down from his horse, leaving a sticky, scarlet smear on the saddle. Then he looped the reins over a fence and went up to the door of the soddie. It was opened before he reached it, whoever was within must have heard the hoof beats approaching their home.

A young woman with a pale, grave face came out. When she saw what kind of state DuBois was in, she didn't waste any time with a lot of foolish questions, but walked over to him briskly and said, 'Here, lean on me. I'll bring you into the house.'

'I'm afraid of getting your dress all over blood, ma'am . . . ' began DuBois.

The woman turned to him fiercely and said, 'You think I set a greater value on this piece of linen than I do a man's life? Do as I bid you and lean on me.'

'Thank you,' he said simply.

There didn't seem to be anybody else at home. It was dark inside the little house, which smelled pleasantly of a mixture of wood smoke and herbs. 'Lay down on the bed there,' ordered the woman, 'I'll tend to your arm.'

DuBois was embarrassed at the mess that he was making in this neat and well kept home. He had dripped a trail of blood across the rush matting on the floor and now he was staining the coverlet of the bed as well. There was a ripping sound and DuBois turned his head to see the woman tearing up some piece of cloth. He started to say, 'Don't trouble to do that,' when for the first and only time in the whole of his life, he fainted.

6

When he came to, DuBois found that he was actually in the bed upon which he had been laying. To his consternation, he discovered that his pants had been removed and realized with horror that this attractive young woman must have undressed him while he was unconscious. He flushed beet-red with mortification at the thought.

Night had fallen while he was out and a brass oil lamp cast its cosy light across the room. The woman was sitting motionless, reading a book by the light of the lamp. She was immediately aware of DuBois, as soon as he opened his eyes, and she stood at once and then walked over to the bed. 'How are you feeling now?' she asked.

'Better, a lot better. I can't take your bed, though. And I'm sorry to put you to the trouble of . . . ' He meant to convey that he was sorry that she had been obliged to undress him. The woman seemed to divine his meaning and for the first time, she smiled.

'If you are referring to taking off your clothes, then you may rest easy. I'm a nurse, it's nothing.'

DuBois looked round the single room. 'You live out here by yourself?'

'No, my husband lives here as well. But he's gone away for a day or two. Don't fret, he would not have had me do otherwise. It's what we are put on this Earth for.'

'You don't know anything about me. My name is DuBois, Gerard DuBois.'

She came over to the bed and took his hand, saying, 'I am very glad to know you, Mr DuBois. My name is Mrs Alice Cavell.'

Pleasant as it was to be laying like this beneath clean sheets and having somebody tend him, DuBois thought that he would be a worthless cur if he didn't set this good woman straight about what type of man he was. He simply could not allow her to shelter him under false pretences. He said, 'You haven't asked how I came to be shot.'

She shrugged indifferently. 'I suppose that it was something in the robbery line.'

'I should tell you about myself,' said DuBois, stunned that she should have the measure of him so quickly. 'It wouldn't be right for me to stay here else.'

'It's no affair of mine. I have sins enough of my own to deal with, without setting up in judgment over other folks. You rest there now and I'll prepare a little broth.'

There didn't appear to DuBois to be much else to say about things. He had never met anybody quite like Alice Cavell and wondered what she and her husband were doing out here in the wilderness. She didn't strike him as being at all like the run of the mill settlers' wives whom he had met in the past. He said, 'Pardon me, Mrs Cavell, but how do you come to be living out here? I didn't see any fields round this place. How do you live?'

'The Lord provides for us,' she said, a note of amusement in her voice. 'And when he can't manage, then the missionary society helps out a little.'

'You're missioners?'

'We are. Medical missionaries, which means that we do a sight more tending to men's bodies than we do looking into their souls.'

Truth to tell, DuBois wasn't overly keen on missionaries and priests, but he thought it would have been churlish to say so in the presence of this obviously good person and so he remained silent.

Alice Cavell brought over a bowl of broth and helped DuBois to sit upright. He saw that his injured arm had been expertly bound up and that it appeared to have stopped bleeding. He said, 'I was afraid that an artery had been severed.'

'No, it wasn't as bad as that. A day's rest should see you ready to ride again.'

111

Fear clutched his heart, as he suddenly recalled that those in pursuit of him might be in the area by now. He couldn't stay here in bed for much longer. Mrs Cavell correctly interpreted his sudden agitation and said, 'You go riding off in less than twenty-four hours and that wound will open up again for sure. You might not be so lucky next time as to find yourself on a nurse's doorstep. I mean it, Mr DuBois, it's life and death, you'll bleed to death if you set out tonight.'

'Well then,' said DuBois ruefully, 'I guess I'll just have to sit back and enjoy this broth.'

★ ★ ★

From when he was a child, Tim Hogan had never had the need for much sleep. All the same, he knew that his horse might not feel the same way and so, at about midnight, he found a sheltered space by a low cliff and decided to rest up for five or six hours. It was cold, but not so cold that he would be unable to sleep out in the open without a fire. He felt the lack of a little extra warmth, but something about that incident with the Indians had put Hogan on his guard. He knew that there was mischief afoot and the less attention he drew to himself out here, the better.

As he lay there, gazing up at the stars, Hogan wondered whether he really wanted to catch up with DuBois at all. Did he wish to see the man hanged for what was, almost certainly, an accidental death? He knew in his heart that this was the last thing he hoped for. Nevertheless, he was a deputy marshal and even if he detested that oaf Granger, he had a duty to his fellow deputy. Maddocks deserved to have his death avenged. It was a troubling conundrum and Hogan fell asleep before he had solved it to his own satisfaction.

Next morning, Hogan rode on to Fort Smith. This had, until the end of the war, been an army post. Now, it was a thriving, bustling town. He knew as he rode in, that things were not all that they should be. There was an air of suppressed panic, with passers-by standing and talking to each other, as though they had received alarming news. In fact, that was precisely what had happened. A month or two earlier, an Indian prophet had come forth in Nevada, a member of the Paiute tribe. This man had proclaimed that God was about to change things in the country and had founded the so-called Ghost Dance movement. In addition to this external manifestation of what was, in effect, a new religion, there was also a secret message. This was that the days of the white man's dominion were numbered and fast drawing to a close.

The alarm in Fort Smith had been caused by the news that a number of homesteads had been attacked the previous night and the inhabitants mercilessly slaughtered. The rumour was that some of the Indians who had taken up the Ghost Dance believed that if the land were to be drenched in the blood of white men, women and children, then the buffalo would return, the white man driven out and things would return pretty much to the way that they had been in the days of their forefathers.

Official messages about some of this had arrived at the marshal's office in Jacob's Lot, but Hogan had understood the focus of the new religion to be up in Dakota, particularly among the Sioux on the reservations there. Word was, Sitting Bull was strong for the Ghost Dance. It was surprising to find the cult erupting as far south as this. It might tie in with the three strangely clad figures whom he had passed on the way here. One thing was for sure, it would make the hunt for Gerard DuBois a good deal harder.

It took some little while to track down the sheriff and when he did, that worthy was engaged in preparing for the defence of the town against what he feared would be a horde of bloodthirsty savages. He showed no interest at all in the whereabouts of the infamous Beau DuBois.

'You think I got time for such foolishness?' asked Sheriff Carter, rhetorically. 'You don't maybe have the idea that I need to save the lives of the folk in this here town?'

'You hear anything as might bear upon an escaped prisoner?' continued Hogan, imperturbably. 'Maybe a robbery or something like that.'

'I mind there was an attempt made at a hold-up on the stage from Fayetteville. Nobody was hurt, bar the man who tried to rob 'em. You might ask the driver 'bout it. Like as not, you'll find him in the Golden Nugget.'

Isaac Thorne was the centre of attention in the Golden Nugget, among those men who were not afraid that the town was about to be destroyed by Redskins. The hold-up of a stage was a rare enough event these days, to give the old man's narrative a certain novelty value and he was capitalizing on this as far as the market would bear

— meaning that he had not had to pay for a single drink so far that day. A natural consequence of this was that by the time Tim Hogan turned up, the old driver was pretty far gone in his cups.

Now shooting the breeze and exaggerating in a barroom is one thing, but telling direct lies to a federal deputy is something else again. When Tim Hogan took the driver to one side and made it plain that he didn't want to hear a heap of tall stories, Thorne caught the drift at once and gave a straightforward and unadorned account of the attempt to rob his stage.

'There was only a-one of 'em,' said Thorne. 'Not a young party either. Maybe fifty or thereabouts. What'd he look like? Well now, he had his neckerchief pulled up over his face, but I seed his hair well enough. Didn't have a hat on, you see. Mass of curls, iron-grey.'

It was enough for Hogan to be sure in his own mind that Gerard DuBois had tried to rob this fellow's coach, only to be shot by a woman and driven off by an old man with a scattergun. There was something indescribably sad about this story and he could only imagine how his childhood friend would have felt about such a reversal.

'Could you tell me exactly where this robbery took place?'

'Follow the road up until you come right to the mountains. Maybe two or three miles from the foothills, that's where he jumped us. Then he ran off to the left of the coach. So if'n you're riding from here, then you might leave the road about two miles before it goes up into the hills and then head right. That'd take you on the same track as that fella took. I mind he'll be dead by now. Either that or a hundred miles from there.'

* * *

In fact, Gerard DuBois was not anything like a hundred miles from the scene of his abortive robbery. He was still tucked up in bed in the Cavells' home — not five miles from where he had been shot.

It had gone very much against the grain for a man like DuBois to lie in bed, while a lady was forced to sleep in a chair. Had he not been so weak from the loss of blood, he would not have countenanced such a scheme in a million years. For all her good nature and kindness though, Alice Cavell was as tough and inexorable as an army drill sergeant. She brooked no opposition and simply took it for granted that her word would be obeyed without question. Since he was a guest in her house, DuBois figured that this was only right and if his hostess was determined to sleep in a chair, then he had no business arguing about the matter.

When he woke the next morning, DuBois knew at once that the arm was healing all right. He couldn't have said how he knew this, because there was still a fair amount of pain. It was healthy ache though, which was indefinably different from the sick pain of an infection. He knew that he would do well enough.

DuBois woke once or twice in the night and then fell asleep again after a little. The lamp was burning all night long and Alice Cavell appeared to be reading or making notes each time he awakened. When he woke properly that morning, she was nowhere to be seen.

One thing was for sure, he would have to make tracks that very day. There was no telling who was after him or how many of them there would be. Apart from his own welfare, he was worried about the good woman who had taken him in. Harbouring an escaped prisoner was a serious offence and he would hate to get Alice Cavell into trouble. DuBois looked round, to see if he could see where his guns had been stowed. It was while he was craning his neck around, that Mrs Cavell entered the house. 'Whatever are you about, Mr DuBois?' she said. He noticed that she pronounced his name with a perfect accent and none of that

'Do boys' business that he had become used to over the years.

'I was just wondering, ma'am, what you have done with my guns?'

'They're in the woodshed,' she said shortly, 'I won't have firearms in my home.'

'I'll be needing them when I leave. I feel that I might be well enough to carry on on my way now.'

'Don't be absurd. You go riding with that arm and the wound will open up again. You need to rest. Lay back in the bed, please.'

DuBois did so, remarking, 'You'd make a good officer, Mrs Cavell. You don't seem to stand much nonsense.'

She smiled and said, 'You are not the first person to make that observation, Mr DuBois.'

Now that the bright, morning sunlight flooded the little dwelling through the windows, DuBois had a chance to see what the place looked like. It was, in essence, no more than a one-room shack. He guessed that Alice Cavell and her husband would have thrown up this place in the course of about a week. Notwithstanding, it was very cosy and pleasant inside. Unlike many such places, there were wooden boards on the floor, instead of trampled earth or puddled clay and the windows were made of glass. These were covered with rush mats. There were prints on the wall as well; coloured rotogravures of Jesus and his disciples.

'Have you lived here long?' asked DuBois.

'Two years. We moved here before the land rush.'

'You only came to spread the word of the Lord? Not to homestead, I mean?'

'No,' she said. 'The Lord called us to minister to the people who live in these parts. They were sorely in need of medical care. My husband is a doctor.'

'You never feel that you'd like to live somewhere a little more comfortable? A city, say?'

This time, Alice Cavell laughed out loud, a silvery glissando which send a little shiver down DuBois' spine. 'I feel that way all the time, Mr DuBois,' she said. 'But I can't desert my post. Why, it would be like a soldier on sentry duty leaving his position without leave. As long as the Lord wants me here, this is where I stay.'

It sounded odd, hearing somebody talk about God in this way, like he was somebody that you just talked to and who told you what you had to do next. DuBois didn't think that he had ever met anybody like Alice Cavell before. All this talk about the Lord was making him feel uneasy, so he said, 'When do you think that your husband is likely to come back?'

'It could be today, it might not be until next week. Things are very restless right now.'

'Restless? How so?'

'You hear about the ghost dancers?'

'Somewhat. Not a great deal, though.'

'There are some Choctaw in this territory who are very strong for the Ghost Dance. They want to cut our throats and think that that will be the route to their salvation.'

'You mean your throat? Why?'

She shrugged impatiently. 'Because we are Christians, I suppose. At any rate, we have a little group of converts, not far from here. They're Seminoles. We've heard that some of the Choctaw have it in mind to kill them and us.'

DuBois sat up urgently. 'Lord, why did you not say so earlier? Fetch me in my guns and I will be ready to help you if need be.'

Mrs Cavell gave him a disapproving look. 'I never yet saw the situation which was helped by firearms,' she said tartly. 'We'll do well enough. Besides, you're in no fit state to help anybody just now.'

★　★　★

In the usual way of things, Tim Hogan did not agonize over his duty. In this case though, he was pulled in two different directions. On the one hand, he knew that he was obliged to find

124

Gerard DuBois and take him back to Jacob's Lot, where he would most likely hang for Maddocks's death. But that would be a low trick to play on a man who had saved his life just recently. For Hogan had no reason to doubt what he had been told, about DuBois knocking up the rifle and spoiling the aim of the man who was about to shoot him. Did he not owe his old friend for that? Besides this there was the reconciliation which he had lately had with the man; the end of over thirty years' worth of resentment. It was a confounding puzzle and no mistake.

In the end, duty won out and Hogan went to hunt out the sheriff again. When he found him, he said, 'What are the chances that you could help me to raise a posse? I'd guarantee payments at the usual rates.'

Sheriff Carter looked at him as though he had taken leave of his senses. 'Are you kidding me? If so, you chose the wrong time, I'll tell you that for nothing.'

'I ain't a-kiddin' you. What makes you speak so? I have a line on the man who tried to knock over the Fayetteville stage. A half-dozen men would do.'

'Yes, I'll be bound they would, only you see, you're not getting them from this town.'

'What's biting you, man? You can spare five or six men, surely?'

'Well but we can't, d'you see? 'Cause I don't know how many Choctaw we got heading this way or if they're the only ones we got to fret about. You hear what's going on in Dakota? I already sent off, asking for troops, but until they get here, not one man from this town's going off to chase your precious outlaw and that's flat.'

All things considered, Hogan couldn't find it in his heart to blame Carter for taking this line. Personally, he thought the whole thing was a gallon of hogwash, but if you're the sheriff, then you have to keep your town's safety paramount. Which was why, after having his midday meal in the Golden Nugget saloon, Tim

Hogan saddled up and rode north by himself. In a way, he wasn't sorry about how things had turned out about the posse. It would have sat ill with him to ride down on a wounded man with six armed men. If there was anything to be done, then it was better by far to do it by himself, just one on one; him and Gerard DuBois facing each other, like real men should do.

7

As the afternoon drew on, it struck DuBois that he had best get himself moving. Like Hogan, he now found himself pulled in two contrary directions. On the one hand, it was his ardent wish to make tracks and get out of the area as soon as he might. Then again, he could not think of leaving an unprotected woman alone, not if there really was trouble in the wind. What sort of cowardly dog would that make him?

As the sun sank towards the western horizon, DuBois asked Mrs Cavell to turn away for a bit, while he pulled on his trousers. She tutted at the idea of his getting out of bed and dressing, but could see that he was determined. When he was dressed, he said, 'I can't leave you until your husband returns. You don't want guns in your home and

I can't say that I blame you. But if there is any sort of attack here, then you won't be able to drive anyone away by waving a Bible at them.'

The woman began to speak, but DuBois forged on and ignored her. 'Fact is, ma'am, I'm not the best man in the world, but I'd never rest easy again if I didn't make every effort to protect you from harm. You pray, if you like, I'm going to strap on my gun, and set watch outside.'

For a second, he thought that he had angered her, but then Alice Cavell smiled again and said, 'You'd risk your freedom and your life for a stranger? I don't know much about you, Mr DuBois, but I am sure that you haven't gone far wrong.'

'That's nothing to the purpose,' he said gruffly. 'You stay here, ma'am, and don't worry about a thing. I am not much of a man, but at least I can take care of somebody who needs my help.'

The woodshed was a little lean-to against the side wall of the soddy.

Inside, was neatly stacked cordwood; on the top of which lay his rifle and gunbelt. He smiled faintly when he realized that he had thought of them as being 'his'. 'I reckon I must have been in the robbery game a little too long,' he muttered softly. 'Getting muddled up about what's mine and what's not.'

DuBois was easier in his mind, once he had a pistol at his hip. The rifle, he set upright against the wall, ready at hand. He hoped that the husband would show up soon for he did not really take to the notion of hanging round here like this. Fighting Indians was all right, but DuBois didn't like the idea of a posse turning up and carrying him off into captivity for ten years or more.

The swollen red globe of the sun was now touching the distant hills and it would soon be twilight. DuBois looked around carefully, scanning every quarter. He could see nobody and nothing that might pose any threat to the Cavells' lonely home. He wouldn't care to live out here like this himself; he preferred the company of his fellow man. While he was musing along these lines and watching the sun set, DuBois saw a lone rider approaching from the west. He stared closely at this apparition; trying to make out if it was an Indian or white man. So intent was he upon the horseman, that he didn't notice a figure gliding swiftly and silently down from the rise of ground on the other side of the house.

Because the rider had the sun behind him, DuBois still couldn't make out whether he was a Choctaw warrior or a harmless traveller. Unwilling to take any chances where the defence of the woman inside the house, he thought it prudent to fetch the rifle from where he had left it. DuBois turned and found himself facing a man who was standing only fifteen or twenty paces away. Instinctively, he drew his pistol. Simultaneously, the other man did the same and the two of them stood there as mutual recognition dawned.

'Where the hell did you spring from, Hogan?'

'Just kind o' tiptoed down from yonder hill.'

'I didn't hear you,' said DuBois. 'You're like a cat.'

'You know what I want, don't you?'

'I can guess. You aim to take me back to a cell.'

'You got that right. You goin' to come quietly?'

'I'm not coming at all, quietly or otherwise.'

The two men faced each other with their guns drawn, both knowing full well that death was waiting near at hand. Neither of them wished to shoot the other, but each was utterly determined to have his own way. It is impossible to say how this matter would have resolved itself, had there not been a sudden and unlooked for interruption.

Hogan and DuBois had eyes and ears for nobody and nothing else; other than each other. They were like a pair of lovers, gazing intently and passionately into each other's eyes. That being the case, they took no notice of the rider who reined in a few yards away and stared in incredulity at the tableau being staged next to his own house. Dr Richard Cavell jumped down from his horse and strode up to the two men, saying, 'What nonsense is this? Put up your guns now, I won't have this at all.'

And still, Tim Hogan and Gerard DuBois gave no heed to anybody except each other. It was not until Alice Cavell came out of the house, greeted her husband warmly and then said, 'Mr DuBois, I am shocked by this!' that he and Hogan turned to the couple outside whose home they were about to begin a bloody gun battle. As though at an unspoken signal, both of them holstered their pistols and Hogan tipped his hat to the lady of the house.

'Sorry to disturb you, ma'am. You too, sir. But I'm a deputy federal marshal and this man is wanted for murder.'

'Murder?' said DuBois, utterly dumbfounded, 'What are you talking about?'

Richard Cavell cut in at this point, saying, 'You fellows can deal with that in your own way at a more convenient time. I need some help right now and it is clear to me that the Lord dispatched the two of you for that very purpose.'

Hogan said, 'Not by a long sight. T'was the marshal's office in Jacob's Lot, over in Missouri, as sent me.'

Richard Cavell might have been a right Godly man and a missioner, but he was still a man for all of that. He said to Hogan, 'Save your foolish jokes for another season, man. We don't have time for them now. Will you men help me or not? If you won't, then you can just clear off my land and go and kill each other out of my sight.'

'What's the case?' asked DuBois.

'You know about the Ghost Dancers?'

'The new Indian religion? What of it?'

'It started out well enough, with their prophet telling them that they must not hurt anybody, they should love their neighbour and so on. Some discontented types have taken up the Ghost Dance though and turned it into a crusade of blood thirst against the white man. Not only that, they're attacking others of their own kind who want to live in peace with the whites.'

'So?' said Hogan. 'What would you have us do about it?'

'My wife and I have helped set up a little settlement, not far from here. It's a medical clinic, with a little church next to it. A group of Seminole have moved nearby and we have a thriving congregation of peaceful Christians.'

'I'm happy to hear on it,' said Tim Hogan. 'But where do me and this fella fit into the scheme?'

'A bunch of Choctaw are heading this way. Say that any Indian who gets too close to white men are like the enemy. Word is, they're likely to slaughter my little flock. You two look handy enough fellows, maybe you could help me to protect my people?'

DuBois was the first to react to this unexpected invitation. He turned to Hogan and said, 'You want we should let the bugles sing truce? Help these folk and then see about our own dispute later?' He reached out his hand. Tim Hogan rubbed his chin thoughtfully and then stretched out his own hand and took that of his former friend.

'Truce then, until we've settled this other business.'

Richard Cavell invited the two men into his home to discuss what needed to be done. There was an army base, just along the state line between the old Indian Territories and Arkansas. If he could persuade his group of families to up tents and move, then they would be able to shepherd them along until they were in the very shadow of the base, where they could reasonably expect to be safe.

'How far from here are your Seminole?' asked DuBois.

'Twelve miles, maybe, from here.'

'What about this army camp?' said

Hogan. 'How far from that are they?'

'Perhaps fifty miles,' said Dr Cavell. 'We must set out at first light in the morning. There's no point trying to move around in the darkness.'

DuBois said, 'What exactly do you want us to do?'

'Do?' asked Cavell in amazement. 'Why, I want you to protect those people with your very lives and see that they are brought to safety. There are women, children and old folk among them. In fact, there are only three able bodied men and one of them is touched in the head.'

Hogan and DuBois exchanged glances, wondering what they had let themselves in for. Tim Hogan said, 'How many people in total?'

'Let me see. There are four very old women, three old men, four younger women and they have seven children between them. Then there are the three younger men. Only two of them will be able to help properly.'

'I make that fourteen adults and

seven children,' said DuBois. 'Is that right?'

Cavell thought for a moment and then nodded.

'Any idea how many of these Choctaw Ghost Dancers might be coming this way?' asked Hogan.

'I heard that a band of about fifty or sixty are moving through the territories in this direction. They have already massacred some of their own people,' Cavell said.

The four of them shared a light meal that evening. There was not a great deal of food in the place, but what they had, the Cavells willingly shared with them. At first, the doctor and his wife wanted Hogan and DuBois to take the bed, while they slept on the floor, but neither man would hear of such an arrangement. In the end, the deputy and the wanted man lay down on the floor, swaddled in various rugs and blankets and the Cavells settled down in their marital bed.

The next day dawned bright and

clear. There wasn't much in the way of breakfast, other than a little cornpone. Alice Cavell would by no means consent to being left out of the adventure, flatly refusing her husband's request to sit tight and wait for his return. She was supported unexpectedly by both Hogan and DuBois. DuBois said, 'I reckon your wife would be more at hazard left here alone than she would be coming along of us all. What do you say, Tim?'

'I should just about say as you're right. We don't know what other Indians have taken up with this Ghost Dance nonsense. At least if Mrs Cavell is with us, we can protect her.'

Her husband looked desperately worried and ran his hand through his hair distractedly. At last he conceded, 'Happen you're right. At least if she's with us, we'll know what's what.' Turning to his wife, he said, 'All right then, my love. Dress up warm, mind. It's turning right bitter.'

The way to the hospital and misson

station was tedious and long. After they had been riding for an hour or so, Hogan said, 'Listen, Doctor, why do you an' your wife live so far from your place? Why don't you live over the shop, as it were?'

'It's a long story,' replied Cavell, 'but it's nothing to the purpose and if you fellows don't mind, I'd sooner focus on what's needful this very day.'

Hogan shrugged indifferently. The little group continued on their way for ten minutes or so, during the course of which time, the Cavells began talking together in low voices. DuBois dropped back a little, so that he and Hogan were riding side by side, a few yards behind the missioners.

'What do you make of all this?' asked DuBois. 'You think there really is a war party heading this way? There hasn't been trouble like that since Geronimo, away over in New Mexico.'

'Hard to say,' said Hogan. 'I been hearin' odd stories, through official channels. There've been a few murders by these Ghost Dancers and some of 'em certainly got a down on Indians who want to live like white folk. It could be true.'

DuBois announced suddenly, 'I didn't mean to kill that other deputy, you know. I struck him on the head with a lump of china. I couldn't have known he would die of it.'

'You're wearing his gunbelt this minute,' remarked Hogan.

'I was escaping. I gave him his chance, didn't hit him from behind or anything of that sort. If he'd have been a little quicker, I might not have been able to strike him.'

'You sayin' it was Maddocks' fault as you lamped him?' asked Hogan, his face a picture of incredulity.

'No, of course I'm not,' said DuBois impatiently, 'I'm saying that you lock up a man and he will try to get away. What do you expect? I'm still sorry that he's dead and I'd have you know I didn't intend to kill him.'

Hogan grunted. He wasn't about to

say so out loud, but he pretty well agreed with this perspective. He'd been ordered to bring Gerard DuBois in, but he certainly didn't feel that the man had behaved in reprehensible fashion. He had done what any other man would have done in similar circumstances; namely, to break free of those holding him prisoner.

Alice Cavell showed herself to be a competent horsewoman. She rode straddling the horse like a man; none of that sidesaddle nonsense. Her petticoats and skirts rucked up, showing more of her leg than was strictly modest, but she was so obviously a God-fearing woman that neither Hogan or DuBois thought any the worse of her for that. There were women who might have invited ribaldry by riding in this way, but Dr Cavell's wife was most definitely not one of them.

The mission station, when once they reached it, proved to be little more than a collection of wickiups and teepees. There was one stone-built structure, which served as Richard Cavell's surgery, and that was next to a soddie which formed a chapel. It was a strange setup and DuBois wondered at the dedication of a man and woman who would devote their lives to living like this — tending to the needy and poor. He had never been much of a one for church-going nor Bible-reading, but he had to admit that the doctor and his wife were true Christians.

As they rode into the little settlement, three or four small children ran out to greet them. They eyed Hogan and DuBois a little warily, but showed no such reserve when rushing up to Alice Cavell. She crouched down and embraced the children, while at the same time looking over their heads and greeting their mothers. A small group of exceedingly ancient looking Indians emerged from the teepees. One of them looked so old and frail that it was a surprise that he was able to shuffle along under his own steam. DuBois said softly to the deputy, 'How in the hell are we supposed to get these people to travel fifty miles over rough country?' Hogan just shook his head. He had no idea himself.

There appeared to be very little in the way of provisions for the journey. There were some flat, round cakes of unleavened bread, a few strips of dried meat and that was pretty much it. DuBois took his old friend's arm and led him away from the others. He said, 'This is madness, Hogan, and you know it as well as I. These people should just stay here and hope for the best.'

'Yeah, I read the case just the same. We set out on a long road with these folk and odds are as not all of 'em'll reach journey's end. Happen we need to speak to the doctor.'

Since their arrival, the whole place had become a beehive of activity, with all the Indians bringing their belongings out of their homes and preparing to break camp. There was no sign of any means of transport such as horses and carts. As far as Hogan and DuBois could see, these people would be walking fifty odd miles with hardly any food and no provision made for the weak.

'Doctor, could we beg a few words with you,' said DuBois. 'It's important.'

'Very well, but it'll have to be quick. There's still much to do before we leave here.'

'That's what we wanted to talk about,' said Hogan. 'We neither of us think it a good scheme to drag these folk through the countryside like this. Let 'em be. They won't, some of 'em, survive this journey.'

'You cowards!' said Richard Cavell angrily and in such a stern voice as to make everybody fall silent and watch what was happening. 'You would back out now, after offering your help? I'm ashamed of you.'

'Nobody's backing out,' said DuBois stiffly, more than a mite irritated to be called a coward so publicly. 'We think that staying here is better for these people.'

'Three days ago,' said Cavell, turning and exchanging a few words in rapid

Seminole with one of the women. 'Yes, she says three days ago, a mission in the Cherokee country was attacked by Choctaw Ghost Dancers. They killed everybody they found there. There were no white people present, they had cut and run. The Choctaw only killed Indians. Now those same people are about twelve hours' ride from here.'

'How'd you know that?' asked Hogan.

'They know,' said the doctor, indicating his little flock. 'Don't ask me how they know, but somehow word has reached them. If they stay here, they'll be slaughtered.'

'You've no doubt about this?' asked DuBois, staring searchingly into the others' faces.

'Not the least. These Choctaw aren't going to attack any white towns, because they know that they'd like as not come up against armed resistance. They hope to make their blood sacrifices among those whose deaths won't matter to us.'

DuBois caught Hogan's eye. Hogan made a grimace; as much as to say, 'fella's got a point'.

'Well then, I guess that's it,' said DuBois. 'We said we'd help and so we will. How are we travelling? Those people are taking down their tents, how do you aim to take them along with us?'

'You never live with Indians, either of you?' asked Cavell.

They both shook their heads.

'Well then, you might not have heard of a travois?'

'The name doesn't bring anything to mind.' said Hogan.

'Come, I'll show you,' said the doctor. 'You will learn something new.

The supporting poles of the dismantled teepees had been lashed together into elongated triangular frames. There were four of these and onto them had been fastened the leather which made up the tents and also the rest of the Indians' belongings.

'I seem to recollect now,' said DuBois, 'that I have seen such things before, although I didn't know what they were called. Surely though, you'll need packhorses to drag them along?'

'Why man,' said Cavell, 'we've four horses. How many more do you want?'

'You want that we should turn our mounts into beasts of burden,' said Hogan, 'and walk alongside them?'

'That's the idea, yes.'

The four wooden frames were secured to the horses who would drag them along. There were two chief advantages to the use of travois in this way. The first was that a horse could pull a much greater weight like this than it could carry upon its back. The other good point about the travois was that a horse drawing one could travel anywhere at all; a wheeled cart is limited to well defined tracks or, at the very least, reasonably smooth ground. Not so, the travois. This can be hauled pretty much anywhere that a horse can go.

It took less than an hour for the Seminole to break camp and be ready to move out. It was agreed that the oldest man and women would ride on the most lightly burdened horse and everybody else would have to walk. DuBois undertook a swift calculation and figured that if the army base was fifty miles away, then it would take at least two days, more likely three, for their party to reach it. He also remembered that Richard Cavell had said that the Choctaws were only twelve hours ride away. The results of DuBois' mathematical exertions were by no means encouraging and he decided to check them over with Hogan.

'If we're all trudging along on foot,' he said, 'and those Choctaw are riding, they're apt to catch up with us by nightfall. Is that how you read it?'

'Yeah. I ain't exactly a whiz at ciphering and suchlike, but I managed to gauge that well enough.'

'What, then?'

'What? Why, I suppose it means that by the time it gets dark, you and me are going to be fighting a bunch of Indians with the odds stacked twenty-five to one against us.'

8

It was not an easy journey. A man of ordinary fitness can walk, on level ground, at perhaps three miles an hour. That means that in the course of an eight or ten hour day, with short rests, such a person might cover a distance of perhaps twenty-five miles. This was the figure upon which Gerard DuBois had based his calculations about the probably length of time needed to reach the army base.

Of course, when you are dealing with old men, women and children, who are making their way across rough and stony ground, these things need to be taken into account if you want to know how long it will take to reach a certain point.

In the event, progress was slower than either Hogan or DuBois had hoped, but more rapid than they feared might be the case. The three younger Indian men, who apparently spoke no English at all, took turns in carrying the younger children.

After they had been on the move for a couple of hours, Alice Cavell, who had been helping the women, came over to DuBois and said, 'We are truly grateful for the help that you and your friend are giving us. You are the answer to our prayers.'

At this, DuBois burst out laughing. 'I have been called many things in my time ma'am, but never yet has anybody described me as the answer to their prayers.'

'You sell yourself short, Mr DuBois. We are all of us the answer to somebody's prayers. What will happen between you and your companion, when once we reach the army's camp?'

'I would not like to venture a guess, ma'am. I hope that it won't come to gunplay, but we are both mighty determined individuals. We must wait and see.'

A little after midday, the group halted for a meal. Hogan came up to DuBois and said, 'There's barely enough food for those people. I'd feel kind o' low taking their vittles from them. Why don't you and me see if we can top up the rations, as it were?'

'I should have thought of it myself.'

The two men told the Cavells what they purposed and walked away from the stopping-place. They would be there for upwards of an hour, it being plain that the children and old people needed a good long rest.

The good thing about the country thereabouts was that it was so sparsely populated still, that many of the animals had not yet had a chance to acquire that wholesome fear of mankind which causes them to flee at the first approach of a human.

Anybody watching the two of them heading up along a track leading to a stream, would never have guessed that they were technically enemies and likely to be fighting to the death at some point over the next two or three days. Both were armed with a rifle as well as a pistol, but neither seemed to fear for a moment that the other would use one of these weapons until they had agreed that the time was come. It was the kind of strange situation which only a strict adherence to the Rattlesnake Code could have brought about. Despite their opposing interests, both men trusted each other implicitly not to make a false move.

'How's that arm of yours?' asked Hogan. 'I see a whole lot of blood on that sleeve.'

'It's better now. Cavell's wife bound it up and I had a day's rest. She's a nurse, I was lucky to stumble upon her.' The two of them carried on up the little valley until they found a suitable spot overlooking a stream.

'See anythin'?' whispered Hogan, as they settled down behind some rocks. 'I can't.'

DuBois shook his head and then froze. He tapped the other man's arm and gestured with a jerk of his head towards the far bank of the stream, where a Pronghorn was tiptoeing delicately to the water's edge, with a view to slaking its thirst. Both men cocked their pieces and very slowly raised their rifles. The antelope was perhaps sixty yards away, but both Hogan and DuBois were tolerable shots at twice that distance. They spoke not a word, but even so, the two shots echoed back and forth from the surrounding rocks almost simultaneously. The Pronghorn leaped convulsively into the air and then flopped over and lay still.

'Which of us hit it, d'you suppose?' asked DuBois.

'I know I did,' said Hogan, 'but I can't answer for you.'

All of a sudden, the two grown men in their late forties jumped up and raced each other to the stream, both keen to prove that it had been his shot which killed the antelope. They splashed noisily through the shallow stream, bounding along like a pair of excited schoolboys.

When they reached the dead animal, it was to discover two neat holes, not an inch apart, in the creature's chest. They sat down by the Pronghorn, laughing contentedly.

'You've not lost your skill with a rifle, seemingly,' said DuBois. 'When we were boys, I recall that no squirrel was safe when you had a gun in your hands. I never saw the like.'

'My ma needed meat for the pot. When you know you'll be goin' hungry if you miss, that's a powerful strong incentive to hit your target. Couldn't afford to waste powder and shot, neither.'

'You were always better than me at shooting,' said DuBois. 'I was so jealous.'

'You was?' Hogan said. 'I never knew that.'

'Got my father's overseer to teach me to shoot. He drilled me and drilled me, 'til I was middling to fair. Never could equal you though.'

'You didn't do so badly just now.'

'That was the war. We all got plenty

of practice and to spare then.'

'Ain't that the truth!'

The antelope was light enough that between the two of them, they were able to carry it back to where the others were resting. The Cavells were relieved that the shots they had heard were a sign of good fortune, rather than the harbinger of an attack by hostile forces.

There looked to be enough meat on the Pronghorn to keep the party going until they reached their destination. There was no time to salt or even wind-dry it and so they simply butchered it and then wrapped up the best parts of meat in leaves. They would be cooking it thoroughly and, given that they hoped only to be travelling for another two days at the most, there should be no problem. It was with a lighter heart that they all set off; whatever else befell them, they were unlikely to starve to death.

Despite the fact that they were in effect handicapped by the slow speed at which the older people were able to walk, DuBois was pleasantly surprised at the distance that they were actually able to cover before nightfall. He had been counting his strides on and off and estimating how far away various landmarks were and the time it took to reach them. According to his calculations, they had travelled some twenty miles by the time dusk fell. 'What would you think?' he asked Hogan. 'We'll make it either tomorrow night or at latest, the following day?'

'I shouldn't wonder. Bar we don't get our throats cut this night by the Ghost Dancers.'

'Yes, I hadn't forgotten that. All the same, we need to sleep. You want that we should take turns to set a watch through the night?'

'No reason we shouldn't get those young men to share sentry-go. Or the doctor, for the matter o' that.'

DuBois shook his head. 'No. I know that you and I won't fall asleep at our posts, but I can't say the same about those others. I trust you, Tim. This is life or death, I'm not going to put my life in the hands of a stranger.'

The deputy looked as though he was about to say something, but then turned away quickly. He was clearly moved that DuBois should speak so casually of trusting him with his life. He, who was supposed to take DuBois back to Jacob's Lot to face the hangman's rope! There was no doubt that life could deal you some damned funny cards on occasion.

It was marvellous to see how swiftly the Seminole were able to pitch their teepees. They undertook the operation in the time it would have taken Hogan and DuBois to tack up their horses. Richard Cavell came over to them while the tents were being erected. He said, 'There is a place for you two in the teepee of the young men.'

'Beggin' your pardon, doctor,' said Hogan, 'but me and my partner here, we've work to do tonight. You an' your wife don't want to wake up in the night with the camp overrun with Choctaw on the warpath. We'll fix up our own arrangements.'

Just as earlier, Hogan had evidently been affected to hear DuBois mention casually that he would trust him with his life, so too was DuBois now moved to hear himself referred to by Hogan as his 'partner'. He too felt a little sad. If Hogan's sadness had been caused by reflecting upon his melancholy duty of taking an old friend to be hanged, for DuBois it was the knowledge that he would in a day or two be compelled to kill his childhood friend. In the meantime though, they were, as Hogan himself had said, partners and there was little point in dwelling on the future. He pulled a dime from his pocket and said to Hogan, 'I'll toss you for first watch.'

When trouble erupted in the night, it was not caused by the Choctaw at all, but by a rather less menacing though none the less unpleasant aspect of human nature among the Seminole whom they were pledged to protect.

DuBois was on first watch, when he heard a piercing shriek; a fearful cry which was cut short and ended in a muffled shout. He at once leaped to his feet and drew his pistol, knowing that some species of devilment was afoot. He moved swiftly and silently to the place where he thought that the scream had come from. To his disgust, he found one of the young men with whom he had shared meat and drink that very evening, attempting to force himself upon one of the mothers.

The light of the moon lit up the scene as clearly as though it were being performed in front of limelight on a stage. Before he even reached the two struggling figures, DuBois could take a good guess at what had happened. The young woman had probably gone away from the teepee to make water and this scoundrel had intercepted her, driven by who knows what carnal lusts. If there was one type of man DuBois loathed above all others, it was those who tried to force themselves upon unwilling women. He walked up and drove his boot hard into the side of the man's head, sending him sprawling in the dirt. Now that the girl's mouth was uncovered, she set up a regular cater-wauling of ululating screams and cries. This roused the whole camp and before long, everybody was up and coming over to see what was what.

After DuBois had set out the case, all present looked at the man grovelling on the ground with repugnance. Hogan was the most vehement in his condemnation. He said, 'What say Gerard, we take him out of camp and shoot him like the dog he is?'

'Sounds good to me,' replied DuBois and, turning to the man, said, 'Come on, on your feet.'

The doctor cut in at this point, saying, 'You men can't be serious? You can't just kill a man out of hand like that.'

'Used to, during the war. Ain't that right, DuBois?'

'It surely is. Best thing, too. Turn him loose now, he'll go off and pull the same trick on some other helpless

woman. Come on, let's get it over with.'
He moved towards the Indian, who was
still sitting on the ground, nursing his
head in his hands. Richard Cavell
moved to block his path. He said:

'I won't have it.'

'I don't want to fall out with you,
doctor,' said DuBois, 'but I will not
carry on with this man in the group.'

'Neither will I,' chipped in Hogan.
'It's not to be thought of.'

'Well then, let him go his own way,'
said Cavell, 'I won't allow you to kill him.'

'Just as you say, sir,' said DuBois,
turning away. Then he whirled round,
quick as a rattlesnake, bent down and
hauled the would-be rapist to his feet.
Holding him securely from behind, he
called, 'Tim, take out a couple of his
toes. Leave him something to remember this night by.'

To Richard and Alice Cavell's unut-
terable horror, Hogan moved to the two
men, drew his gun and then, bending
low, shot off the big toe of the Indian's
left foot. DuBois released the man and

then gave him a kick, saying, 'Get moving. You're lucky to escape with your life.'

The young Indian had, during the journey, given both Hogan and DuBois the impression that he neither spoke nor understood English. Whether or not he did, he definitely understood now what was required of him, because he limped off into the night. Alice Cavell came up to the men who had executed this summary justice and said harshly, 'That was a barbarous thing to do!'

'It was no more than he deserved,' said Hogan, 'he was lucky we let him off so light.'

DuBois added, 'Of all the crawling creatures on the earth, there's none so low as those who abuse and mistreat women. I'm half minded to follow him this minute and finish off the job.'

The doctor's wife looked from one man's face to the other, finding on both an implacable determination. She turned away in disgust. The Indians, who probably thought that the man had been treated with kid gloves and let off with no more than a slap on the wrist, moved back to their teepees. 'I don't think that Mrs Cavell is none too keen on us,' said Hogan quietly.

DuBois laughed. 'You may be right. I'm only sorry now we didn't kill him anyway.'

'With luck, he'll get blood poisoning and die alone in the wilderness.'

DuBois' face brightened. 'Yes,' he said, 'I hadn't thought of that.'

The next morning, the atmosphere between the Cavells, Tim Hogan and Gerard DuBois was a little frosty. This was more than made up for though, by the way in which the Indians unbent towards the two men. Before this, they had viewed Hogan and DuBois with reserve and a certain amount of suspicion, regarding them perhaps as wandering gunslingers recruited because they would be handy in a fight. Having seen how angry the men had been about the assault on an unprotected woman changed their opinion. The old women came up and took Hogan's hand before they set off, talking to him unintelligibly in Seminole. As for DuBois, the younger women made a point of smiling shyly at him, whereas before, they had just ignored his existence.

While the teepees were being packed away and converted into travois for the journey, Hogan and DuBois wandered off out of earshot of the others. When they were a little way away, Hogan said, 'I would o' thought as those Ghost Dancers might o' caught up with us by now.'

'Same thing was on my mind. If they're riding and we're walking, I would have expected them last night. You think Cavell will know anything about the business?'

'I don't see any harm in asking him.'

Richard Cavell was still disposed to be a little cold towards the men who had behaved with such violence only a few hours ago, but he listened carefully to what Hogan and DuBois had to say. Then he said, 'I dare say they've stopped to perform their circle dance, which many of us call the 'Ghost Dance'.'

'Dancing? That shouldn't hold 'em up for too long,' said Hogan. 'I can't see that being the cause o' the delay.'

'How much do you men know about this Ghost dance business?' asked Cavell.

'Nothin' at all to speak of,' replied Hogan. 'What about you, DuBois?'

'Much the same,' admitted DuBois.

'It's supposed to be a religion of peace,' said Cavell, 'started by a Paiute called Wovoka, away over in Nevada. He sometimes goes by his English name, which is Jack Wilson.

'Three months ago, he dictated a letter to be sent to the tribes here in the territories. Wait a minute.' Cavell went over to his horse and took something from the saddlebag. It was a folded sheet of paper and he brought it back to where Hogan and DuBois waited. He said, 'Listen, I'll read it to you. Wilson gave this message to some Choctaw from near here who went and asked him what to do about the loss of the Indian Nations. 'When you get home you must make a dance to last five days. Dance four nights in a row and then on the fifth day dance all night until dawn, when you must all bathe in the river and then go to your homes. I, Jack Wilson, love you all and my heart is full of gladness for the gifts which you brought me. When you get home, I shall give you all plenty of rain for your crops. I will give you good spirits and also good paint. Grandfather says, when your friends die, do not mourn them. Do not tell the white people about this. The dead are here again and alive. I do not know when they will come to you. Maybe this fall or perhaps in the spring. When that time comes, everybody will be young again and you will all have plenty of food. The white people will go away and the buffalo will return.''

'Sounds like a sermon such as a Christian priest might preach,' observed DuBois. 'All that about the dead coming back and everybody being young again and having full bellies. No offence meant to you, sir.'

'That's how my wife and I read it as well, but some people say that there is a double meaning to phrases about the white people going away. Some of the Choctaw certainly are taking it so. It could also be that Wovoka gave them another message, by word of mouth.'

'Begging your pardon sir, but what has this to do with us now?' said Hogan. 'What bearing does it have on when we may expect these Choctaw to come down on us?'

'All those who are taking part in this business have sworn to give up the white man's ways. That means not drinking his whiskey or using his guns either. All the warriors who are hot for this new faith have stopped using anything that we introduced them to. They also carry out the circle dance for eight or twelve hours every day. It's their way of communing with their God. I'd say that that might slow them down a bit in their pursuit of us.'

When they were alone again, Hogan said to his old friend, 'Well, we had to go all round the houses, but I reckon as Cavell's right about it. Those men chasing us are wasting their time by stopping to dance for hours at a time. I'd say it gives us a good edge.'

'It's still going to be touch and go whether we get to the army base before they catch up with us.'

9

Both Hogan and DuBois felt a good deal easier in their minds when they were on the move again. It was irksome not to be riding, but at least they were able to set a fairly stiff pace on foot and urge the others to keep up with them. This naturally meant that the two of them were often ahead of the others, stopping from time to time to bawl at the rest, telling them to hurry up. It was only to be expected that striding side by side, the two men fell into conversation about the way of things. They had both noticed the decline in morals in recent years and the increasing difficulty of finding men who could be trusted.

'That business last night,' said DuBois, 'that wasn't the only case of such beastliness that I've come across lately.' He gave a brief account of the man he has shot in Arkansas for trying to assault his neighbour's daughter.

Hogan shook his head in disgust. 'You'd think real men would be ashamed to carry on so. You know, I don't recall nothing of that sort when I was a younger man.'

'That would be because they knew what the result would be,' said DuBois grimly. 'When a man knows that tricks of that sort will end with his being hanged or, at best, having his balls cut off by some angry men, it tends to act on him so that he controls himself more.'

'It ain't just the fear of punishment, Gerard. There's less sense of honour around than there once was. You see it all the time. Men lie and cheat, they don't half of 'em seem to know when they're behaving dishonourably.'

'Yes,' said DuBois. 'It's because in the old days, we made the rules ourselves and kept them ourselves. You think back to the Rattlesnake Code. Nobody had to police that, because it was something men knew within them.

171

When some bigwig up in Washington makes laws, it's not the same. I don't set mind to half of the laws made by lawyers a thousand miles away.'

'Which,' remarked Hogan dryly, 'is what has led you to your present pass.'

DuBois laughed at that. Then he turned round and shouted to the stragglers, 'What's wrong with you people? You want to get scalped by the Choctaw? For the Lord's sake keep up, can't you?'

By 1890, the days of the outlaw were more or less over in most parts of the country. There were still one or two bands of men like Beau DuBois' gang, but roaming road agents and robbers were unusual. However, in the former Indian territories, there were still a fair number of wanted men, those who either could not or would not settle down and live lives more in keeping with the times. Some of these were men who had committed such dreadful crimes that they would never be left alone and allowed to fade into obscurity. As long as the territories were the exclusive preserve of the Indians, such men often found refuge there. Once they were opened up for settlement though, eventually to become part of the state of Oklahoma, it was all up with these desperate characters. They no longer had any hiding place and knew that it was a matter of time before the law caught up with them. Until that time, they scraped out wretched lives, keeping as far away from the towns and newly homesteaded areas as they possibly could. It was the merest chance which caused five such men to cross the path of the little party seeking sanctuary near the army base that November of 1890.

Mick Doolan and Frank Harper were train robbers, hold-up artists and murderers. There were warrants for them in four states and for the last year, they had been hiding out in the territories, hoping against hope that they would eventually be forgotten. There was little enough reason to expect this.

During their last robbery, a little

affair in Texas, Doolan and Harper had ended up killing a mother and her two young children. If they were ever caught in that state, the chances were that a lynch mob would save everybody the cost of a trial. The other three men who had picked up with them were also depraved types who, unless some miracle should chance, were fated to end their days dangling at the end of a rope as well. On this particular day, the five men had nothing much in mind, other than to make enough cash money to enable them to eat properly for a week or two. The pickings were getting mighty lean. They ran into the party that Hogan and DuBois were guarding, purely by the vagaries of fortune. Riding round a bend in the gulley through which the road ran, they almost collided with Hogan and DuBois as those men chivvied along the older members of their group.

When Doolan saw the Indians and their white companions, he summed up the case in his head very swiftly. Only a bunch of Christians would bother to help these pitiful cases along the road: the old, the lame and mothers with small children. At the very least, there looked to be four healthy horses that could be traded on and should enable the five of them to sustain themselves for a while. To say nothing of what pickings there might be in the way of jewellery, cash and perhaps a woman or two. Yes, thought Mick Doolan, things were suddenly looking up!

The Indians stopped, sensing trouble and Richard Cavell then moved from horse to horse, halting them as well. The five riders who were blocking the road, had spread out in such a way as to make it plain that they did not intend anybody should pass. Cavell came hurrying up and said to the men on horseback, 'What's to do?'

'We was wondering who you folk are and where you're bound for?' said Doolan.

'I'm a medical missionary and these people are in my charge. I'm leading them to safety. Please don't obstruct us.'

'Missioners, hey?' said Doolan, pleased that he and his boys had unwittingly stumbled across such easy prey. 'What about your two friends here?' He indicated Hogan and DuBois and addressed them, saying, 'You men missionaries as well?'

Hogan rubbed his chin, meditatively. 'No, I couldn't rightly say as I'm a missionary. What about you, Gerard?'

'Why no, I don't recollect when last I was in church or read the Good Book. I'm no missioner either.'

For the first time since encountering the little expedition, Mick Doolan felt the stirring of a faint doubt. Cavell looked harmless enough; he wasn't even carrying. But these other two were looking at him and his men in a queer way, that he did not at all care for. He said, 'You ain't missioners? Who are ye then?'

'Well now,' said Hogan, 'I'm a deputy federal marshal. My badge is in my bag.'

Before the men had had a chance to digest this startling intelligence, DuBois added, 'And I'm Beau DuBois. You boys might have heard of me. I'm here to tell you that if you trouble us in any way, then any blood shed will be upon your own heads. Mark what I say.'

Without turning round, Hogan called out, 'Doctor Cavell, take your flock back a ways. Least 'til we see which way this is going to end.' Cavell and his wife began to shoo the Indians back and off the road.

'We neither of us have any interest in you men,' said Hogan. 'Turn back the way you came and we'll let you go.'

Frank Harper spat in the dirt. 'You say what, you cowson?' he said. 'You'll let us go? You crazy or what? Throw down your guns and we might let you live.'

DuBois could have wished that he had his rifle near to hand, but there was no point thinking so. He said, 'We have warned you. You know what we purpose. What will you have?'

Harper brought up a sawn-off scatter-gun that he kept tucked into a makeshift scabbard on the front of his saddle. He didn't get the chance to use it though, because Hogan drew at once and shot him dead. As he fell from his horse, Harper twisted round helplessly and, in his death agonies, squeezed the trigger of the gun he was gripping, sending a charge of buckshot into the man next to him.

As soon as Hogan fired, DuBois decided that presenting the men in front of them with a sitting target would not be the smartest move in the world. During the confusion that resulted from Hogan's shooting of Frank Harper and the subsequent wounding of another man by Harper's scattergun, DuBois sprinted forward, until he was behind the remaining three riders. Then he shot Mick Doolan in the back. This was not at all a cowardly act; once the shooting had begun, Doolan knew that he must look to his defence. It was up to him to protect himself as best he was able.

One of the other men fired at Hogan, but his horse was bucking and rearing in terror from the sudden eruption of gunfire. The bullet went wide and so Hogan drew down on the man and shot him through the heart. The only man who had so far taken no part in the battle, turned his horse and spurred it on, cantering off the same way that he and his friends had come from. DuBois sent a shot after him, but didn't bother to aim too hard.

'You all right, Tim?' shouted DuBois.

'Never better,' replied his friend. 'That's one o' the shortest gunfights I ever seen!'

Mick Doolan and Frank Harper were both stone dead, as was the other man that Hogan had shot. The one who had stopped the charge from Harper's scattergun was laying in the road, breathing rapidly. He had caught the full force of the shot to his stomach and parts of his bowels were protruding from a hole the size of a saucer. Hogan reached down and removed the man's pistol from its holster.

'You're dying,' Hogan told the man

bluntly. 'You got any kin as you want us to carry a message to?'

'Hell, no,' said the man, 'I ain't seen my family these ten year or more.'

'We wouldn't o' shot any of you,' said Hogan, 'not if you'd given us the road.'

'I don't think it matters now,' said the wounded man in a matter of fact voice. At that point, Dr Cavell and his wife came over to see if there was anything that could be done for the injured man. The doctor examined the wound gravely and then turned away in despair. His wife said;

'Would it help you if I were to say a prayer?'

The man laughed and then started coughing. DuBois observed with a horrified fascination that the loop of intestines which was sticking out of the wound, moved in and out as the man coughed. When he had finished coughing, the effort of which had cost him dear and left him pale and shaking, the man said, 'I'd as soon not, lady. I'd feel a right hypocrite at this time o' my life.

But if one of you boys could spare me a smoke?'

Hogan put a little tobacco into his pipe and lit it. Then he sat next to the man, holding the pipe for him. After a few refreshing lungfuls, the man gave a sigh of contentment, closed his eyes and died.

Hogan stood up and said, 'Come on you people, let's get movin'.'

Alice Cavell said fretfully to DuBois, 'Did you have to kill them? Could you not have just wounded them or shot their weapons, rather than shooting to kill?'

'You mean shooting their guns out of their hands?' asked DuBois. 'That's all a heap of nonsense, ma'am. It might answer in a dime novel, but in a case like this, it's kill or be killed. You should be glad that we killed them, before they sent us to hell.'

She looked at him with dislike and walked away.

An incident of that nature, where death is faced down and a man comes out of it the same as he went in, which is to say still breathing and alive, gives an added spice to life. Both Hogan and DuBois felt pretty bucked by taking on five men and neither one of them sustaining so much as a scratch. As they walked along, the two of them discussed the gunfight and debated what the other side could have done to alter the outcome.

'It was that damned fool pulling out that shotgun that sealed it for them,' said DuBois. 'Killed his friend into the bargain. As soon as I saw him reaching down like that, I knew he was going to draw. If they'd just pulled pistols on us, things might have turned out differently.'

'Still and all,' said Hogan, 'it was neat work, the two of us seeing off five men like that. It's been a while since I've done anything of the kind.'

'Truly? I would have thought that in your line of work, you would always be facing up to long odds of that sort.'

'No, most of being a deputy is

serving papers, executing warrants and suchlike. There's not all that much gunplay. Not these days.'

And still there was no sign of the Choctaw who were supposed to be bearing down on them. It might, as Richard Cavell said, be because the men were involved in some strange religious rites, but DuBois was beginning to think that the whole thing was a snipe hunt and getting to the army camp would be no more hazardous in reality than taking a trip to visit relatives in another part of the country.

After they had rehashed the shootout, both Hogan and DuBois stopped talking and walked along for a spell in companionable silence. Both were thinking of what was waiting for them in no more than twenty-four hours.

There was no question of DuBois going tamely to what looked certain to be his death for the murder of Deputy Maddocks. He would sooner die in a clean gunfight than kick out his life in a noose. There was, equally, not the slightest possibility that Timothy Hogan would turn a blind eye to DuBois escaping. Such an action was not in his nature, He had said that he would bring back his man and that is just precisely what he would do, or die in the attempt. Which meant that after they had fulfilled their agreement with the Cavells and delivered them and their converts safely to the vicinity of the army camp, Hogan and DuBois were bound to enter into a struggle from which they could not both be expected to emerge alive. This was a sobering thought, which the closer they came to their destination, the more did it occupy the minds of both Hogan and DuBois latterly to the exclusion of all else.

There was something more to be considered as well: since meeting at the Cavells' home, the two men had in some strange way rekindled the friendship of their youth. They had measured each other up, looked at what the years had done and were, on the whole, satisfied with each other. Both were men of strong principle, both were honourable, according to their lights, and both were utterly determined to plough their own furrow in life and have their own way. Now there was the added complication that they had fought together in a deadly battle, looking out one for the other and routing odds of better than two to one. You tended to feel an even stronger affinity for a man who had shared such an adventure with you. The truth was, Gerard DuBois and Timothy Hogan had decided that they liked each other very much and under other circumstances, they would have become firm friends. All this made for a regular conundrum, the solution to which was not at all clear to either of them.

While they were walking along quietly, both sunk in their thoughts, Richard Cavell came up behind them and said, 'I would be an ungrateful wretch if I were not to give you my hearty thanks for saving us back there. I could have wished that it had been achieved without killing, but still, I am thankful.'

'I'd sooner manage things without killing myself, doctor,' said Hogan. 'One way or another, there was going to be blood let, and to speak plainly, I'd sooner it was another man's and not mine.'

'What will you two men do when we arrive at the base?'

Since this was just precisely what the two of them had been considering, Hogan and DuBois looked a little taken aback by the question.

Cavell said, 'Don't look so surprised. It would be a miracle if this hadn't been on your minds. Have either of you any thoughts on the matter?'

DuBois glanced at his friend and said, 'I should think that we have both of us had thoughts about it, Doctor Cavell. But without wishing to cause any offence, it's by way of being a private matter and we'd as soon not discuss it with others.'

Cavell looked from one to the other.

Both DuBois and Hogan had neutral expressions upon their faces, which suggested either that they had nothing of great import on their minds just now or that they were determined that nobody other than they themselves should know anything of their inner turmoil. There was no point in pressing the question further and so the doctor said, 'I hope that you will neither of you end by harming the other.'

The day was drawing to a close and still there had been no sign of the Choctaw who were supposedly on their trail. What they did come across was a small, temporary encampment of Seminole, some of whom were evidently known to their travelling companions. Although neither Hogan nor DuBois knew this part of the country at all well, if what Cavell had told them was accurate, they were likely to reach the army base within another twenty-four hours at the most. Left to themselves, the two men escorting the Indians would have been inclined to snatch a couple of hours' sleep and then march on through the night. It was clear though that the children and old folk would not be up to this and so they would need to pitch camp properly for the night. It was while they were looking for a good spot, that they came across the tents of this wandering band of Seminole.

There were only a half-dozen or so teepees and they were grouped in a rough circle around a cheerful fire. When the party that Hogan and DuBois were escorting first came into sight, there were cries of alarm from those gathered round the campfire, but as soon as those in the encampment recognized fellow Seminole, the mood lightened. It was not altogether clear to Cavell what the relationship was between the two groups — whether one of kinship or simply acquaintance. What soon became apparent though was that there was room for all of them around the fire and that those who had pitched their tents there were ready and willing to share what they had with the newcomers. This made for a convivial atmosphere and everybody was soon chatting and laughing. The young man whom Cavell had referred to as 'touched', was made especially welcome and given the best place in front of the fire. To the white men, he was just a simple soul who was a little touched in the head, but to the Indians he was a man of some account. Again, the white men could not make out if this was because he was related to somebody of significance or just because the Indians saw him as being possessed by spirits. Either way, he was transformed for the evening into a man of consequence.

After he had eaten his fill, both of the broiled meat of the antelope which he and Hogan had killed and also of the meat and drink freely offered by the other Seminole, DuBois walked away from the fire and found himself a boulder to sit on. He needed to be alone.

As he read the case, Gerard DuBois was now faced with the unappealing choice of either being killed in a painful and degrading fashion or of murdering a friend. Neither prospect was an attractive one. Once they reached safety, he and Hogan would face up to each other. He could submit tamely to being taken back to Missouri to hang, but he was damned if he would follow that path. Then again, he could shoot his old friend and make his escape. There was also the slender chance that Tim Hogan would be able to kill him, but he didn't find that at all likely. Hogan might be the better shot, but he was unlikely to be as quick on the draw as DuBois. In contests of that kind, where it was life and death, the victory almost invariably went not to the man who was better at target shooting on a range, but to the one who could throw as much lead around in the shortest possible time. DuBois was pretty confident that that would be him.

There was of course a third road, but it was one which he scorned to take. That would be to abandon these helpless people now, leaving his old friend to guard them by himself, while he, DuBois, scooted off into the hills and put as much space between himself and Hogan as he could. For a moment, he weighed up the benefits of this course of action in his head, before thrusting the idea from him savagely. Imagine that! He, Beau DuBois, promising to protect the weak and helpless and then walking out on women and children because he was afraid for his own skin. Why, he would never be able to look at himself in a mirror again if he took that road. He would be a man who had placed a few extra years of life above honour and courage. It wasn't to be thought of!

10

The day dawned bright and clear, with scarcely a cloud in the sky. Both Hogan and DuBois were up before the others, stamping their feet and slapping their arms round their bodies in an effort to get warm. Because there were so many of them camped here, they had decided the previous night that it was worth the risk for them both to get a good night's sleep.

DuBois was walking in a slightly lopsided way, favouring one leg over the other. It was hardly noticeable, but Hogan spotted the irregular gait and asked straight out, 'Why're you limpin'?'

'It's that damned rheumatism. The cure up at Eureka Springs worked well enough, but all this sleeping out in the open has brought it right back again.'

Hogan didn't say anything for a space and DuBois wondered if he was about to make some joke about the business. Instead, he said soberly, 'We're neither of us as young as we once were, DuBois. I can't say as I'm all that comfortable myself, sleeping on the ground these days. I don't have the rheumatics, but I surely get more aches and pains after a night in the open than when I was a young man.'

They stood there for a few seconds, both conscious of their mortality. Then DuBois said in a low voice, 'Is there no way out of this? Couldn't we just part after we reach this sanctuary? I'm only asking that you turn your back, nothing more.'

Hogan appeared to mull this proposal over, before saying regretfully, 'It can't be done. I never yet took a bribe or allowed any personal feeling to affect my work. I engaged to fetch you back to Missouri and that's what I aim to do.'

'One of us will die. You know that, as well as I do.'

Hogan shrugged. 'It could be so. But what will be, will be. I'm not going to bend the law or give up my duty on that account.'

'You are one stubborn bastard, you know that?'

'I think it has been remarked upon in the past,' said Hogan, with the ghost of a smile on his lips. 'You should hear what my boss has to say on the subject, he waxes quite eloquent about it.'

There was little more to be said and so they went to rouse the camp and get their own people ready to move out.

Before they set off, Richard Cavell spoke to two of the old men. Then he came over to where DuBois was assisting in securing a travois to one of the horses. 'Mr DuBois, I have been consulting with one of our band. He tells me that as far as he is able to calculate, we should reach the base before sunset today.'

'What about these other Indians? Are they coming with us or not?'

'No,' said Cavell. 'They have business of their own. I don't rightly know what, but they're going on their own way now. Have you and your friend reached any sort of accommodation?'

'Not really, no,' said DuBois sadly. 'It's a damnable thing. There's to be bloodshed one way or another.'

'I hope not, I'm sure.'

Once they were all on the move again, Hogan and DuBois resumed their positions at the head of the straggling line of horses, men, women and children. As before, they called out regularly to urge on the faint and weary, doing their best to set a smart pace which would guarantee their arrival in the vicinity of the army camp before darkness fell.

'What do you think?' asked Hogan. 'We'll make it before we meet those Ghost Dancers?'

'I surely hope so. I've seen enough action in the last few days to last me for a good long while.'

Hogan laughed softly and said, 'I'm surprised at that. I mean with you being an outlaw and all.'

'Ah, you will have your joke. But mostly we try to avoid gunplay, where we can. You know what it's like. I'll warrant it's the same on your side of the road. If you can deal with a problem without pulling iron, I'll be bound that that's how you'd prefer it.'

'You got that right.'

The land was fairly smooth and level now and they were making better time than they had the previous day. The two oldest Indians, one man and one woman, rode on the lightest of the travois and although it could not have been the most comfortable mode of travel, it was certainly quicker than if they had been tottering along under their own steam. The terrain thereabouts was so flat, that they were able to see pretty much as far as the horizon. They were, as far as they were able to see, the only travellers.

At midday, they all stopped for a rest. There was some cornpone and a few slices of cooked meat from the previous night's meal, but when they had finished that, that was it. There were no reserves to fall back upon. The same thought was in both the Cavells' minds and also those of their two escorts; what

196

will we do if we don't reach the army camp this day? The Indians didn't seem to be troubled about this at all. They had seemingly put their faith either in Jesus or the white folk. Either way, they appeared to expect any problems to be solved by others, rather than by any exertions of their own.

The children took their mood from the adults around them, the older ones darting around playfully as they made their way across the plain. Once they had all stopped for a time, two or three of the children came up to Hogan and DuBois. They had obviously been told by their mothers that these two white men were their saviours and they showed by gestures that they wished to examine the pistols carried by the two men. Both of the men were human enough to feel flattered by this attention and willingly drew their pistols and exhibited them to the young Indians. This proceeding roused Alice Cavell to anger and she spoke sharply to the children, sending them back to their mothers.

'They wasn't bothering us none,' protested Hogan. 'I don't mind having young'uns round me.'

'Well it bothers me,' said the doctor's wife, 'seeing innocent children being taught that there is something wonderful about firearms. It might tickle your vanity, but you're training them up to be killers in the future.'

'A man can own a gun, without using it to kill anybody,' remarked DuBois, mildly; at which Mrs Cavell turned sharply and fixed him with a disapproving eye.

'And has that been your own experience, Mr DuBois?' asked the woman. 'You have known many men who wave guns about and then don't go on to shoot their fellow creatures?'

DuBois was lost for words, which caused Hogan to say, 'She got you there and no mistake, DuBois!'

She turned to the deputy and said, 'You're just as bad, sir. How many people have you shot? You think that guns are such fine things?'

DuBois chuckled. 'Now she's got you

as well, Hogan.'

'I don't know anything much about you two men. I can guess enough, though. But one thing I do know for certain sure is that I am not about to watch the pair of you corrupt innocent children, by teaching them a love of guns.' Having delivered herself of this opinion, Alice Cavell turned on her heel and walked away.

'I call that right ungrateful,' said DuBois, smiling. 'If it hadn't been for those nasty guns of ours, that bunch of bushwhackers would have made short work of her and her precious children.'

'Ah, you know what women are like,' said Hogan. 'They're always in a mood over something. If it hadn't been our guns, it would have been 'cause our fingernails were dirty or we hadn't of combed our hair or some other foolishness.'

The two of them stood there for a moment, united in masculine disapproval of fussy femininity. The longer that they spent in each other's company, the more that the two of them reverted to the carefree and easy ways of their childhood. They acted like tonics on each other. Both were sorry to think that later that day, the odds were that they would not both still be alive and breathing.

By late afternoon, they found themselves walking towards a line of low hills. Cavell walked rapidly to catch up with them, where they marched at the head of the column and said, 'I'm told that the army base is just behind those hills. How long would you say it would take us to reach them?'

'Perhaps two hours?' suggested DuBois.

'That's about what I thought,' said the doctor. 'Thank the Lord, we're almost home and dry. We'll make it yet.'

'Maybe,' was all that Tim Hogan would say. He and DuBois were both looking towards the hills and thinking that you couldn't hope for a neater spot for an ambush.

The army base towards which the group was heading was really little more than rows of tents which housed two squadrons of cavalry. They had only been there for a month, having been dispatched as a precaution when the Ghost Dance began to take hold in the Indian Territories. The three hundred men lived in what was like a little town. A deep ditch had been dug all around and the earth banked up to form a protective wall. This had been topped with sharpened logs. The men stationed in the base were on a war footing, although they had not actually seen any action yet. Their role was to guard the border between the former Indian Nations and Arkansas and ensure that any disturbances did not spill over into the more settled lands to the north and east.

Although the events of that winter were later dignified with the name of the Ghost Dance War, it amounted in reality to little more than a series of minor skirmishes, most of which took place in Dakota, rather than as far south as the territories. So far that

November, the very presence of the cavalry seemed to have acted as a discouragement to any kind of activity by local disciples of the new cult.

The hills through which the group of Indians passed with their white escorts were low and criss-crossed with easy trails. Once they reached the highest point, it was possible to see the Ozarks, lying remote and clear on the far horizon. Nearer at hand was the army base which lay about three miles from them.

'You think those soldiers will provide food and water for these poor devils?' DuBois asked his friend.

'You think as that there Mrs Cavell would take 'no' for an answer?' laughed the other. 'I'll take oath that she'll obtain lodgings for them inside the camp itself.'

'Yes, she has what you might call a strong personality.'

It was as they walked down the gentle slope which led out of the hills and onto the plain before them that DuBois felt the first intimations of disaster. He said to Hogan, 'You hear anything out of the ordinary?'

'I can hear horses' hoofs. What of it, there's a cavalry base yonder.'

'Yes, better than two miles from here. Listen carefully.'

DuBois stopped dead in his tracks and called loudly, 'Everybody stop. Just stop moving so that me and my partner can listen.'

It took a few seconds for Cavell to stop the horses and for the Indians to stand still. By that time, there was no mistaking the sound of hoof beats near at hand. 'I surely hope that that's a cavalry patrol!' said Hogan and no sooner were the words out of his mouth, than from the space between two of the nearby hills thundered fifty or sixty riders. The hope that these would turn out to be troopers of the US cavalry was a vain one. The men who were bearing down on them wore thick pelts of buffalo and they were carrying lances and bows. The Choctaw had caught up with them at last.

Neither Gerard DuBois nor Tim Hogan wasted any time in reproaching themselves for having been lulled into a false sense of security. It was fairly obvious that the Choctaw had arrived in the hills before them and simply bided their time until the party of Seminole arrived. Nor was there any point in asking what was behind this determination of theirs to kill this bunch of women, children and old men. The two of them darted at once to the travois upon which their rifles were carried and snatched them up.

'Get those people into a small group,' shouted DuBois. 'Get them together, for God's sake.' Then he knelt down, worked a round into the breech and took careful aim at the lead rider. He fired at once and was pleased to see the man he had shot fall from his horse. DuBois was aware of Hogan firing as well and the oncoming riders swerved away in alarm at the shooting which appeared to take them by surprise. Perhaps they had assumed that only unarmed missionaries would be prepared to walk alongside these vulnerable and helpless people. Whatever the reason, the Choctaw seemed taken aback to find that they were coming under accurate and sustained fire.

The body of horsemen split in two as it came towards them. This was a great relief, because DuBois feared that they might just ride them down. The attackers probably wished to know how many men were equipped with firearms and as they rode by, DuBois could see the warriors peering at them, counting the shots. As they galloped past, several of the riders threw their lances into the densely packed group. One missed entirely, another inflicted a flesh wound on one of the old men, but the third, whether by luck or judgment, took one of the women right in the chest. She fell down and her child began wailing in terror.

Although they were keeping their eyes fixed on the Choctaws who, once they were a safe distance away had turned their horses and were showing every sign of being about to charge towards them again, both Hogan and DuBois heard the sharp, metallic note of a cavalry bugle in the distance. They had little time to ponder the significance of this however, because the riders had started back towards them. This time, they did not charge straight at the huddle of frightened Seminoles, but veered off and began circling around them. DuBois fired a couple of times, once hitting a horse and the other time missing anything as far as he could see. Some of the warriors began firing arrows up in a high arc, while still riding. There was no possibility of accurate shooting under such circumstances, but a few of the arrows found their marks.

'This is sheer murder,' cried DuBois. 'If we don't take action, they'll just kill us all without even needing to come close and hazard their own selves.'

'What would you have?' asked Hogan, reloading his rifle and firing again.

'Why, to take the attack to them of course! Are you game?'

'I reckon I am at that,' said Hogan. 'Pistols?'

'And rifles, both,' replied his friend. Before the Cavells had any idea what they had in mind, Hogan and DuBois leapt to their feet and drew their guns. Then, their rifles clutched in their left hands, they ran straight at the riders, firing their pistols at them as they did so.

It was such a completely mad and unexpected move that the riders circling them were thrown momentarily into confusion. Some turned and fled, while others reined in suddenly, causing those behind to crash into them. Then, disaster struck. They were only a dozen yards from the Choctaws and almost certain to be skewered by arrows in another moment, when Gerard DuBois tripped and fell face forward onto the dirt. One rider saw his opportunity and rode forward, his lithe, springy lance balanced in his hand. He halted his horse, so that he should be able to aim well and then hurled the lance unerringly at the prone figure.

The Cavells saw what happened next and afterwards Richard Cavell was to relate the incident any number of times in sermons, to illustrate Jesus' teaching of 'Greater love hath no man than this, that a man lays down his life for his friends'. Having emptied his pistol, Timothy Hogan was helpless to prevent his friend from receiving the spear in his back, as he lay winded. So he did the only thing he could think of to prevent DuBois' death. He ran forward as the Choctaw brave hurled the deadly missile and received it in his own chest. It was impossible to say whether this was his intention, or if he was hoping to catch it instead. Whatever Hogan's motive, the fact was that the lance, which was tipped with a razor-sharp obsidian head, thudded straight into him and knocked him to the ground.

As Hogan went down, there another bugle call, much nearer this time and a second later, fifty troopers from the nearby camp crashed into the Choctaws, scattering them and sending the Indians fleeing in disarray.

The noise of the battle faded away as DuBois got to his feet. He saw his friend at once, lying on his back, with the fearsome weapon embedded in his chest. He ran to Hogan, but it was too late. The lance had plunged straight through his old friend's heart.

DuBois knelt down by the side of the man he had known for over thirty-five years. In death, Tim Hogan still had that same, faded look of pure Georgia Cracker about him. He didn't look as though he had died in pain; his face still wore that same, patient and shrewd look that DuBois remembered so well from their childhood. It had been decades since he had cried, but remembering his younger self now and the good times that he had shared with this man long ago, DuBois felt hot tears running down his cheeks. He knew that he had never had a real friend since he and Hogan had been boys together and now that friendship was over, severed by the one fact of life from which we can never escape: our own mortality.

A gentle hand touched his shoulder and DuBois looked up. It was Alice Cavell and he suddenly felt ashamed to be seen like this by a woman, with tears streaming down his face. She sensed his embarrassment and said, 'You should be proud of feeling so much for him. It's not a matter for shame.'

'He was a good friend,' was all that he could say.

11

The closing act of the Ghost Dance War was not played out until another six weeks had passed. It took place not in the Indian Territories, but way up in South Dakota at a little place called Wounded Knee Creek. By that time, the affair at the army encampment in the territories had almost been forgotten. There had, after all, been only a handful of casualties, none of whom were soldiers. Only one white man had died; a federal deputy called Timothy Hogan.

It took over a week for news of Hogan's death to filter back to Jacob's Lot. When it did, nobody could figure out what the hell he had been doing, fighting Indians over in the territories. A few messages passed back and forth between the army and the Marshal's Office in Missouri, but by that time the

Cavells and their little flock had moved on and there was no other source of information. They never did find out what Hogan had been up to. Because Marshal Granger had insisted on his deputy leaving in pursuit of DuBois before writing a report, nobody ever knew about the little farm owned by DuBois under the name of Butler either. Beau DuBois was still wanted for the murder of a federal deputy marshal and in the fullness of time, men turned up at his home in Shelby; just on the off-chance that he would have gone to ground with his wife and son. They had themselves gone by that time, though, without leaving a forwarding address. The trail was stone cold and the whereabouts of Gerard 'Beau' DuBois never were established. It was guessed that he too had been killed in the unrest of the Ghost Dance War.

Four days after the death of Tim Hogan, there was a knock at the door of Ned Archer's farmhouse. When his wife went to see who it was, she gave a cry of pleasurable surprise. 'Why Mr Butler, I declare that this is the first time I ever did know you to come calling on a neighbour. How did you get on in Eureka Springs?'

'It did me a power of good to begin with ma'am, but the pain started again soon after I left. Might I speak to your husband?'

'Oh, listen to me, keeping you talking on the threshold. Mr Archer's in the barn. You come in now and I'll go fetch him.'

'There's no need ma'am,' said DuBois, 'I'll just step over there to catch him. It's been a pleasure talking to you.'

Ned Archer was chopping wood in the barn. He looked genuinely pleased to see DuBois, which made the other feel good. He didn't waste words, saying, 'Archer, when last I was here, you said you'd help me out if need be. Does the offer still stand?'

'Of course it does. What can I do for you?'

'That spread of mine. If farmed

properly, would it be big enough to support a small family? Say a man, his wife and a child?'

'Why yes,' said Archer, looking a little puzzled. 'What do you have there? A hundred acres?'

'About that, yes.'

'Well I've about the same here and it keeps me and my family just fine. Mind, it's hard work, but you wouldn't be afraid of that, I suppose?'

'I might be a little out of practice, but that can soon be remedied.'

'What's this favour you're seeking?' asked Ned Archer. 'You want to borrow money or a plough or something?'

'Lord, no. I would just like your counsel and advice on the farming business, nothing more than that.'

Archer looked at him strangely. He said, 'Butler, that's just what any neighbour would do for a friend. It's how we live. That ain't a favour, it's what men do, one for the other whenever there's need. You're a strange one and no mistake, to come begging for such a favour.

I'd do it for any man.'

For some reason, DuBois felt shamed by this man's honest and open delaration. He said, 'It's a while since I lived and worked among ordinary folks, Archer. You must forgive me.'

'That's nothing. Who's this family that you say will be living on your land, anyway?'

'Why, mine, of course.'

'You have a wife and child? You kept that quiet!'

'You'll be meeting them soon enough. I hope that we can be good neighbours.'

As he rode over the hill to his own land, DuBois reflected that he had lived the last quarter of a century according to one fixed and immutable set of rules: the Rattlesnake Code. This would not answer, now that he was about to settle down and live like any other man in a civilized part of the country. He would need to learn a whole new way of behaving and dealing with his fellow man. Archer had given him the first of these new rules, that neighbours helped each other when necessary. There would be others to pick up, but he was sure that he would manage well enough.

We do hope that you have enjoyed reading this large print book.

Did you know that all of our titles are available for purchase?

We publish a wide range of high quality large print books including:
Romances, Mysteries, Classics
General Fiction
Non Fiction and Westerns

Special interest titles available in large print are:
The Little Oxford Dictionary
Music Book, Song Book
Hymn Book, Service Book

Also available from us courtesy of Oxford University Press:
Young Readers' Dictionary
(large print edition)
Young Readers' Thesaurus
(large print edition)

For further information or a free brochure, please contact us at:
Ulverscroft Large Print Books Ltd.,
The Green, Bradgate Road, Anstey,
Leicester, LE7 7FU, England.
Tel: (00 44) **0116 236 4325**
Fax: (00 44) **0116 234 0205**

BANDIT'S GOLD

Alex Frew

When Joe Flint meets Matt Harper and Pete Brogan, he is enticed by their tales of gold and mystery. They tell of a legendary Mexican leader who funded his reign during the Civil War through a criminal network. Drawn in by the promise of fortune, he follows his new friends. But along the way, they are attacked. Flint learns too late that he has put himself in the hands of madmen. Will he find his fortune? Will he even get out alive?